THE KING IS
ALWAYS ABOVE
THE PEOPLE

THE KING IS ALWAYS ABOVE THE PEOPLE

STORIES

DANIEL ALARCÓN

RIVERHEAD BOOKS

NEW YORK

2017

RIVERHEAD BOOKS
An imprint of Penguin Random House LLC
375 Hudson Street
New York, New York 10014

The following stories have been published previously, in slightly different form:
"The Thousands" (*McSweeney's*); "The King Is Always Above the People," "The Provincials,"
and "The Bridge" (*Granta*); "Abraham Lincoln Has Been Shot" (*Zoetrope*);
and "República and Grau" (*The New Yorker*).

ISBN 9781594631726

Printed in the United States of America
1   3   5   7   9   10   8   6   4   2

Book design by Gretchen Achilles

FOR THE THREAD™

CONTENTS

THE THOUSANDS

1

THE BALLAD OF ROCKY RONTAL

5

THE KING IS ALWAYS
ABOVE THE PEOPLE

15

ABRAHAM LINCOLN
HAS BEEN SHOT

37

THE PROVINCIALS

49

EXTINCT ANATOMIES

107

REPÚBLICA AND GRAU

115

THE BRIDGE

133

THE LORD RIDES A SWIFT CLOUD

179

THE AURORAS

189

ACKNOWLEDGMENTS

241

THE KING IS
ALWAYS ABOVE
THE PEOPLE

THE THOUSANDS

THERE WAS NO MOON that first night, and we spent it as we spent our days: your fathers and your mothers have always worked with their hands. We came in trucks, and cleared the land of rock and debris, working in the pale yellow glow of the headlights, deciding by touch and smell and taste that the land was good. We would raise our children here. Make a life here. Understand that not so long ago, this was nowhere. The land had no owner, and it had not yet been named. That first night, the darkness that surrounded us seemed infinite, and it would be false to say we were not afraid. Some had tried this before and failed—in other districts, on other fallow land. Some of us sang to stay awake. Others prayed for strength. It was a race, and we all knew it. The law was very clear: while these sorts of things were not technically legal, the government was not allowed to bulldoze homes.

We had until morning to build them.

The hours passed, and by dawn, the progress was undeniable, and with a little imagination one could see the bare outlines of the place this would become. There were tents made of tarps and sticks. There were mats of woven reeds topped with sewn-together rice sacks, and sheets of pressboard leaning against the scavenged hoods of old cars. Everything the city discarded we'd been saving for months in preparation for this first night. And we worked and we worked, and for good measure spent the last hours of that long night drawing roads on the earth, just lines of chalk then, but *think of it, just think* . . . We could see them—the avenues they would be— even if no one else could. By morning, it was all there, this ramshackle collection of odds and ends, and we couldn't help but feel pride. When we finally stopped to rest, we realized we were cold, and on the soft slope of the hill, dozens of small fires were built, and we warmed ourselves, each taking comfort in it, in our numbers, in this land we had chosen. The morning dawned pale, the sky scoured clean and cloudless. "It's pretty," we said, and yes, the mountains were beautiful that morning.

They still are. The government arrived before noon and didn't know what to do. The bulldozers came, and we stood arm in arm, encircling what we had built, and did not move. "These are our homes," we said, and the government scratched its febrile head. It had never seen houses like ours—our constructions of wire and aluminum, of quilts and driftwood, of plastic tarps and rubber tires. It came down off its machines to inspect these works of art. We showed the government the places we'd made, and eventually it left. "You can have this land," it said. "We don't want it anyway."

The newspapers wondered where the thousands had come from. How we had done it. And the radio asked as well, and the television sent cameras, and little by little we told our story. But not all of it. We saved much for ourselves, like the words of the songs we sang, or the content of our prayers. One day, the government decided to count us, but it didn't take long before someone decided the task was impossible, and so new maps were drawn, and on the empty space that had existed on the northeastern edge of the city, the cartographers now wrote *The Thousands*. And we liked the name because numbers are all we ever had.

Of course, we are many more than that now.

THE BALLAD OF
ROCKY RONTAL

⇒ 1 ⇐

Let's say your given name is Adrano Rontal, but they call you Rocky. Let's say you're a poor boy growing up in a poor city in a poor region of a very rich country. The richest in the world, or so they tell you. Let's say there's no evidence of that, at least not any that you've seen.

You have five brothers and a little sister. You're not the oldest, but you are the bravest. Brave, even though you're small. Brave, even when you shouldn't be.

Let's say the welfare check comes on the first and the fifteenth. Your father gets his cut first. For whiskey. No one sees him until night falls . . . And then, it isn't your older brothers who protect your mom.

Instead, it's you. Let's say they dress you in layer after layer of clothes: extra sweaters, long-sleeve shirts, jackets, an ad hoc suit of armor, so stiff you can barely bend your arms. And your father, he beats you with a nightstick, like the kind cops use. And still you don't cower.

Life has a way of punishing brave boys like you. Life has a way of making brave boys like you punish themselves. Particularly here. Where you live. You already know that.

One night your father gets carried away. He locks you in the closet, and your mother spends the night sleeping with her back to the door, to protect you.

In the morning, she sneaks the keys out of your father's pocket. Let's say she opens up the closet. And you're caked in blood.

And so she kicks him out. A not insignificant act of bravery for a young woman with little education and few prospects, suddenly alone, with six children to feed.

You don't know it yet, but you're full of guilt. Full of hate.

Within a year, your older brothers are in juvenile. Now you're ten years old. Now you're the man of the house.

Let's say one day a social worker comes by to check on you and your brothers. There's no food in the pantry. You're humiliated. You and your baby sister and your younger brothers are sent to a children's shelter. You escape that same night and come home, but it's your mother who convinces you, with tears in her eyes, to go back. "Don't you wanna be with your younger brothers?" "Yes, jefita." So you spend three months there, in a foster home, across the street from a methadone clinic. You recognize the junkies when they come by. You know them from the neighborhood. "Hey, Rocky," they say. You can't wait to go home.

You promise yourself you'll never let the food run out again.

So when you come home, you start stealing. The first time you ever get busted it's for breaking into a fruit stand. But before long you move on to bigger things. Let's say you burglarize houses, taking anything that can be sold, but paying special attention to the food. You fill your father's old duffel bag with cereal, with bread. You're obsessed with the pantry. Obsessed with keeping it full. A week before the food runs out, you're already in motion.

And then: at thirteen you've got your first .38. It's the year you graduate to boosting cars. Let's say you get a list, three or four a week. Make, model, year, color. You're going to school now and then, but it's like you're not really there. You have other business.

At fifteen, you get picked up and sent to juvenile, like your brothers before you. You see friends from the neighborhood, tough, unsmiling boys just like you. You meet others, from all over California. And this is the first time you realize what you are. Or rather, this is the first time you realize what the world thinks you are.

Let's say you're sitting in a group meeting when the counselor calls you a gang member.

You're offended. You hang around with people of the same cloth, the same experience, the same sufferings. These are your friends, like family. You don't think of yourselves as gang members, but of course, technically, that's what you are.

And let's say you embrace the label.

When you get out, you start doing robberies. Holding up liquor stores, convenience stores. Let's say you carry a gun, and every night you wave it in the faces of frightened cashiers. You don't just take the bills; you take the change too. And at the end of the night, when you come home, let's say you empty your pockets, slipping these coins under the pillows of your little brothers and your sister. It'll make them smile when they wake up. They'll know it was you who left the coins, even if they won't know where they came from.

2

This is a story of three terrible crimes. The first is your childhood.

Here's the second. Let's say you're seventeen when a crew of Sureños come up from Los Angeles. They're called Vicky's Town, or VST, and it isn't long before they're tagging in the neighborhood.

"Kick on back," you say. You let it be known. This is how wars begin.

Your house is sprayed with bullets one night when you aren't home. Your mother tells you, and then immediately regrets it. You know what to do. She begs you not to. Let's say you do it anyway.

This is it. It's two in the morning when you drive to your victim's house. Let's say you shoot him at close range with a sawed-off pump shotgun. Let's say his mother and his little sister are in the house.

You don't let your mother come to the trial. Let's say you tell your brothers not to let her near the courthouse, not under any circumstances. But she's your mother, and she comes. Years later, she'll tell you, "You were always a good boy, mijo . . ." And you'll find it astonishing she could say that, much less believe it.

But she does.

Let's say the day she comes to the courthouse is the day the coroner testifies about your victim's wounds. You'll remember this for a long time. He's on the stand, giving a detailed medical account of what happened, and your mother is sitting behind you, hiding her face with both hands. And on the other side of the courtroom, your victim's mother is doing the same.

It's the first time you feel ashamed of what you've done. If someone had intervened, right then, let's say you could've been saved.

You're sentenced to twenty-seven years to life.

You're inside a year and a half when your little sister and a friend of hers disappear. It's 1982, and this is the third terrible crime. Your sister's name is Renee and her friend is named Nancy, and they're both thirteen years old. Let's say they were last seen on the avenue, getting into a car with two men. The two girls are found a week later, facedown in a ditch on the outskirts of town.

Let's say you wonder if your sister paid for what you did. Now you're sending out messages, lists of people you want executed. You don't know who did it, so you want them all dead. You want to see bodies stacked up high, a monument to the pain you're feeling.

Let's say you want to murder the world.

And then one of the men is caught and tried, and sentenced to death. And one day you see him, across the yard, separated by two fences, and you get him a message. *One day,* you tell him, *after the system kills you, I'll get out. And I'm going to kill your family.* You mean it. He knows you mean it, and that's the only satisfaction you have.

Let's say every time you come across someone inside, someone who hurt a child, you think of him. And you make them pay.

But the other man who killed Renee and Nancy gets away. Let's say his name is Reyes. He gets away and stays away. Let's say he vanishes somewhere in Mexico.

One decade, two decades, three. Reyes has a life. He gets married. He has children. He's divorced. He marries again.

And all that time, while the man who raped and murdered your sister is walking the streets, you're in prison, and your hatred is something sharp in your chest. Something darker, more toxic than rage. You don't let your family call you. You don't let them reach you. This is something you have to do alone.

⇒ 3 ⇐

Let's say sometime during your second decade in prison you begin to think about the true meanings of simple words. Words like *compassion. Understanding. Consideration. Forgiveness.* Simple words.

No one you grew up with could have defined any of them.

Let's say one night, on the block, you wake up wondering who you are. What right you have to hurt anyone. Is this an eye for an eye? Didn't you take a life?

You ask yourself why you turned out the way you did, but you know you'll never arrive at a satisfying answer. But let's say you resolve to stumble on.

Let's say in 2012 you're released. All told, you've spent thirty-two years inside.

Let's say you emerge into a world that's disappointingly familiar. Your town is the same, only more so. The violence you loosed has become routine, and the kids have learned from you. Perfected what you taught them. Your mother's dead. Your homies are dead. Some of your brothers have died too.

You go around town and tell everyone you've hurt that they don't need to be afraid of you anymore. It's a long list. You visit the mother of the boy you killed.

The last time you saw her was in the courtroom, when you were on trial for the murder of her son. Now she has salt-and-pepper hair, and sits in an armchair, both her hands resting atop a cane, her head bent down toward the floor. She's still afraid of you. You get on one knee, and with all your might you give her an explanation of why you did what you did.

You don't ask for forgiveness. You accept responsibility. When you're done, she clears her throat, and says that no one in her family had anything to do with Renee's death.

She's afraid of you.

She says she's seen you in the neighborhood talking to the youngsters. She knows you're trying to make amends. Then she says she forgives you. It takes your breath away.

Then she changes the subject: "What else have you been doing?" she asks.

"Construction," you say.

"So do you know how to fix cabinets?"

"Yeah, señora."

"That's good, mijo. Do you know how to fix fences?"

"Yeah, señora."

"That's good, mijo," she says. "So now you're gonna fix my cabinet and my fence."

⊯ 4 ⊱

And then you get a call. Alfredo Reyes has been caught. Before you know it, they've brought him back from Mexico, and the trial has begun.

Let's say you weren't prepared to see the paunchy, middle-aged man before you, his slouch, his thinning hair. He tells the court that no, he never spent much time thinking of Renee or Nancy. Very rarely did he remember what he'd done.

You spent decades inside remembering what he did.

"It was consensual anyway," Reyes tells the court, and your heart rate quickens.

"It was the other guy who killed those girls," he says, and you clench your fists.

But you aren't the person you were. And still. Let's say you spent years dreaming of killing this man. And now you've sat through weeks of his trial, watching him. Thinking, repeating to yourself: *Compassion. Understanding. Consideration. Forgiveness.*

These words you've taught yourself. Words that suddenly seem meaningless again.

And then you find yourself, at your sister's grave site, full of rage. And then you find yourself climbing a wall across the street from the courthouse, and up a ladder, to the roof of an old theater. Let's say from here you can see the garage where the bus pulls in from the county jail. From here you could have a clean shot.

He says it was consensual. He described it.

And let's say you find yourself on the roof, holding a rifle, the feel of it like an old friend. Let's say you can imagine the bullet hitting Reyes, and the image of him falling is so clear in your mind, it's like a movie you've watched a thousand times.

You're watching, you're waiting for the bus to come.

What happened on the roof of that theater?

Let's say you saw the man you used to be.

THE KING IS ALWAYS
ABOVE THE PEOPLE

IT WAS THE YEAR I left my parents, a few useless friends, and a girl who liked to tell everyone we were married, and moved two hundred kilometers downstream to the capital. Summer had limped to a close. I was nineteen years old and my idea was to work the docks, but when I showed up the man behind the desk said I looked scrawny, that I should come back when I had put on some muscle. I did what I could to hide my disappointment. I'd dreamed of leaving home since I was a boy, since my mother taught me that our town's river flowed all the way to the city. My father had warned me, but still, I'd never expected to be turned away.

I rented a room in the neighborhood near the port, from Mr. and Mrs. Patrice, an older couple who had advertised for a student. They were prim and serious, and they showed me the rooms of their neat, uncluttered house as if it were the private viewing of a diamond. Mine would be the back room, they said. There were no windows. After the brief tour we sat in the living room, sipping tea, beneath a portrait of the old dictator that hung above the mantel. They asked me what I was studying. All I could think of in those days was money, so I said economics. They liked that answer. They asked about my parents, and when I said they had passed on, that I was all alone, I saw Mrs. Patrice's wrinkled hand graze her husband's thigh, just barely.

He offered to lower the rent, and I accepted.

The next day Mr. Patrice recommended me to an acquaintance who needed a cashier for a shop he owned. It was good part-time work, he told me, perfect for a student. I was hired. It wasn't far from the port, and in warm weather, I could sit out front and smell the river where it opened into the wide harbor. It was enough for me to listen and know it was there: the hum and crash of ships being loaded and unloaded reminded me of why I had left, where I had come to, and all the farther places that awaited me. I tried not to think of home, and though I'd promised to write, somehow it never seemed like the appropriate time.

We sold cigarettes and liquor and newspapers to the dockworkers, and had a copy machine for those who came to present their paperwork at the customs house. We made change for them and my boss, Nadal, advised those headed to customs as to the appropriate bribe, depending on what item they were expecting to receive, and from where. He knew the protocol well. He'd worked for years in customs before the dictator fell, but hadn't had the foresight to join a political party when democracy came. His only other mistake in thirty years, he told me once, was that he hadn't stolen enough. There had never been any rush. Autocracies are nothing if not stable, and no one ever thought the old regime could be toppled.

We sold postcards of the hanging, right by the cash register: the body of the dictator, swaying from an improvised gallows in the main plaza. In the photo, it is a cloudy day, and every head is turned upward to face the expressionless dead man. The card's inscription reads *The King Is Always Above the People*, and one has the sense of an inviolable silence reigning over the spectators. I was fifteen when it happened. I remember my father crying at the news. He'd been living in the city when the man first came to power.

We sold two or three of these postcards each week.

In the early mornings I wandered around the city. Out in the streets, I peppered my speech with words and phrases I'd heard around me, and sometimes, when I fell into conversations with strangers, I would realize later that the goal of it all had been to pass for someone raised in the capital. I never pulled it off. The slang I'd picked up from the radio before moving was disappointingly tame. At the shop I saw the same people every day, and they knew my story—or rather, the one I told them: a solitary, orphaned student from a faraway city neighborhood. "When do you study?" they'd ask, and I'd tell them I was saving up money to matriculate. I spent a good deal of time reading, and this fact alone was enough to convince them. The stooped customs bureaucrats in their faded suits came in on their lunch break to reminisce with Nadal about the good old days, and sometimes they would slip me some money. "For your studies," they'd say, and wink.

There were others—the dockworkers, always promising the newest, dirtiest joke in exchange for credit at the store. Twice a month one of the larger carriers came in, depositing a dozen or so startled Filipinos for shore leave. Inevitably they wandered into the shop, disoriented, hopeful, but most of all thrilled to be once again on dry land. They grinned and yammered incomprehensibly and I was always kind to them. *That could be me,* I thought, in a year, perhaps two: stumbling forth from the bowels of a ship into the narrow streets of a port city anywhere in the world.

I was alone in the shop one afternoon when a man in a light brown uniform walked in. I'd been in the city three and a half months by then. He wore his moustache in that way men from the provinces did, and I disliked him immediately. With great ceremony he pulled a large piece of folded paper from the inside pocket of his jacket and spread it out on the counter. It was a target from a shooting range: the crude outline of a man, vaguely menacing, now pierced with holes. The customer looked admiringly at his handiwork. "Not bad, eh?"

"Depends." I bent over the sheet, placing my index finger in each paper wound, one by one. There were seven holes in the target. "What distance?"

"At any distance." He asked, "Can you do better?" Without waiting for me to respond, he took out an official-looking form and placed it next to the bullet-riddled paper man. "I need three copies, son. This target and my certificate. Three of each."

"Half an hour," I said.

He squinted at me and stroked his moustache. "Why so long?"

The reason, naturally, was that I felt like making him wait. And he knew that. But I told him the machine had to warm up. Even as I said this, it sounded ridiculous. The machine, I said, was a delicate and expensive piece of equipment, newly imported from Japan.

He was unconvinced.

"And we don't have paper this size," I added. "I'll have to reduce it."

His lips scrunched together into a sort of smile. "But thank God you have a new machine that can do all that. You're from upriver, aren't you?"

I didn't answer him.

"Which village?"

"Town," I said, and told him the name.

"Have you seen the new bridge?" he asked.

I said I hadn't, and this was a lie. "I left before it was built."

He sighed. "It's a beautiful bridge," he said, allowing himself to indulge briefly in description: the wide river cutting through green rolling hills that seemed to stretch on forever.

When he was done reminiscing, he turned back to me. "Now, listen. You make my copies, and take your time. Warm up the machine, read it poetry, massage it, make love to it. Do what you have to do. You're very lucky. I'm happy today. Tomorrow I go home and I have a job waiting for me at the bank. I'll make good money, and I'll marry the prettiest girl in town, and you'll still be here, breathing this nasty city air, surrounded by these nasty city people." He smiled for a moment. "Got that?"

"Sure," I said.

"Now, tell me where a man can get a drink around here."

There was a bar a few streets over, a dingy spot with smoky windows that I walked by almost every day. It was a place full of sailors and dockworkers and rough men the likes of whom still frightened me. I'd never been, but in many ways, it was the bar I'd imagined when I was still back home, plotting a way to escape: dark and unpleasant and exciting, the kind of place that would upset my poor, blameless mother.

I took the man's target and put it behind the counter. "Sure, there's a bar," I said, "but it's not for country folk."

"Insolent little fucker. Tell me where it is."

I pointed him in the right direction.

"Half an hour. Have my copies ready." He noticed the plastic stand with the postcards of the dictator's hanging and scowled. With his index finger, he carefully flicked them over, so that they all tumbled to the floor.

I let them fall.

"If I were your father," he said, "I would beat you senseless for disrespect."

He shook his head and left, letting the door slam behind him.

I never saw him again. As it happened, I was right about the bar. Someone must have disliked the looks of him, or maybe they thought he was a cop by the way he was dressed, or maybe his accent drew the wrong kind of attention. In any case, the papers said it was quite a show. The fight started inside—who knows how these things begin—and spilled out into the street. That's where he died, head cracked on the cobblestones. An ambulance was called, but couldn't make it down the narrow streets in time. There was a shift change at the docks, and the streets were filled with men.

SHORTLY AFTER MY ENCOUNTER with the security guard, I wrote a letter home. Just a note really, something brief to let my parents know I was alive, that they shouldn't believe everything they read in the newspapers about the capital. My father had survived a stint in the city, and nearly three decades later, he still spoke of the place with bewilderment. He went there shortly after marrying my mother, and returned after a year working the docks with enough money to build the house where I'd been raised. The city may have been profitable, but it was also frightening, an unsteady kind of place. In twelve months there he saw robberies, riots, a president deposed. As soon as he had the money together, he returned home, and never went back. My mother never went at all.

In my note I told them about the Patrices, described the nice old couple in a way that would put them both at ease. I would visit at Christmas, I promised, because it was still half a year off.

As for the target and the dead man's certificate, I decided to keep them. I took them home the very next day, and folded the certificate carefully into the thin pages of an illustrated dictionary the Patrices kept in their front room. I tacked the target up on my wall so that I could face it if I sat upright in bed. And one night a storm rolled in, the first downpour of the season, and the rain drumming on the roof reminded me of home. I felt suddenly lonely, and I shut my left eye, and pointed my index finger at the wall, at the man in the target. I aimed carefully and fired at him. It felt good. I did it again, this time with sound effects, and many minutes were spent this way. I blew imaginary smoke from the tip of my finger, like the gunslingers I'd seen in imported movies. I must have killed him a dozen times before I realized what I was doing, and after that, I felt a fidelity to the man in the target I could not explain. I would shoot him every night before sleeping, and sometimes in the mornings as well.

One afternoon not long after I'd sent my letter, I came home to find the girl from my hometown—Malena was her name—red-faced and teary, in the Patrices' tidy living room. She had just arrived from the country, and her small bag leaned against the wall by the door. Mrs. Patrice was consoling her, a gentle hand draped over Malena's shoulder, and Mr. Patrice sat by, not quite knowing what to do. I stammered a greeting, and the three of them looked up. I read the expressions on their faces, and by the way Malena looked at me, I knew immediately what had happened.

"Your parents send their best," said Mrs. Patrice, her voice betraying grave disappointment.

"You're going to be a father," her husband added, in case there had been any confusion.

I stepped forward, took Malena by the hand, and led her to my room in the back without saying a word to the Patrices. For a long while we sat in silence. There had never been anyone besides me in the room, except for the first time the Patrices had shown me the place. Malena didn't seem particularly sad or angry or happy to see me. She sat on the bed. I stood. Her hair had come undone, and fell over her face when she looked down, which, at first, was often.

"Did you miss me?" she asked.

I had missed her—her body, her breath, her laughter—but it wasn't until she was in front of me that I realized it.

"Of course," I said.

"You could've written."

"I did."

"Eventually."

"How long?" I asked.

"Four months."

"And it's—"

"Yes," Malena said in a stern voice.

She sighed deeply, and I apologized.

Malena had news—who else had left for the city, who had gone north. There were weddings planned for the spring, some people we knew, though not well. As I suspected, the murder of the security guard had been a big story, and Malena told me she herself hadn't been able to sleep, wondering what I might be doing, whether I was all right. She'd visited my parents, and they'd tried to convince her not to travel to the city, or at least not alone.

"Your father was going to come with me."

"And why didn't he?" I asked.

"Because I didn't wait for him."

I sat beside her on the bed, so that our thighs were touching. I didn't tell her that I'd met the victim, about my small role in his misfortunes, or any of that. I let her talk: she described the small, cosmetic changes that our town had undergone in the few months I'd been away. There was talk of repainting the bridge. I nodded. She was showing already, an unmistakable roundness to her. I placed the flat of my palm against her belly, and then pulled her close. She stopped talking abruptly, in mid-sentence.

"You'll stay with me. We'll be happy," I whispered.

But Malena shook her head. There was something hard in the way she spoke. "I'm going home," she said, "and you're coming with me."

It was still early. I stood up, and walked around the tiny room; from wall to wall, it was only ten short paces. I stared at my friend in the target. I suggested we see the neighborhood before it got too dark. I could show Malena the docks or the customs house. Didn't she want to see it?

"What is there to see?"

"The harbor. The river."

"We have that river back home," she said.

We went anyway. The Patrices said nothing as we left, and when we returned in the early evening, the door to their room was closed. Malena's bag was still by the front door, and though it was just a day bag with only one change of clothes, once I moved it, my room felt even smaller. Until that night, Malena and I had never slept in the same bed. We pressed together, and shifted our weight, and eventually we were face-to-face and very close. I put my arm around her, but kept my eyes shut, and listened to the muffled sounds of the Patrices talking anxiously.

"Are they always so chatty?" Malena asked.

I couldn't make out their words, of course, but I could guess. "Does it bother you?"

I felt Malena shrug in my arms. "Not really," she said, "but it might if we were staying."

After this comment, we were quiet, and Malena slept peacefully.

When we emerged the next morning for breakfast, my landlords were somber and unsmiling. Mrs. Patrice cleared her throat several times, making increasingly urgent gestures at her husband, until finally he set down his fork and began. He expressed his general regret, his frustration and disappointment. "We come from solid people," he said. "We are not of the kind who tell lies for sport. We helped settle this part of the city. We are respectable people who do not accept dishonesty."

"We are church people," Mrs. Patrice said.

Her husband nodded. I had seen him prepare for services each Sunday with a meticulousness that can only come from great and unquestioned faith. A finely scrubbed suit, shirts of the most pristine white. He would comb a thick pomade into his black hair so that in the sun he was always crowned with a gelatinous shine.

"Whatever half-truths you may have told this young lady

are not our concern. That must be settled between the two of you. We have no children ourselves, but wonder how we might feel if our son was off telling everyone he was an orphan."

He lowered his eyebrows.

"Crushed," Mrs. Patrice whispered. "Betrayed."

"We do not doubt your basic goodness, son, nor yours . . ."

"Malena," I said. "Her name is Malena."

". . . as you are both creatures of the one true God, and He does not err when it comes to arranging the affairs of men. It is not our place to judge, but only to accept with humility that with which the Lord has charged us."

He was gaining momentum now, and we had no choice but to listen. Under the table, Malena reached for my hand. Together we nodded.

"And He has brought you both here, and so it must be His will that we look after you. And we do not mean to put you out on the streets at this delicate moment because such a thing would not be right. But we do mean to ask for an explanation, to demand one, and we will have it from you, son, and you will give it, if you are ever to learn what it means to be a respectful and respectable citizen, in this city or in any other. Tell me: Have you been studying?"

"No."

"I thought not," Mr. Patrice said. He frowned, shook his head gravely, and then continued. Our breakfast grew cold.

Eventually it would be my turn to speak, but by then I had very little to say, and no desire to account for anything.

Malena and I left that afternoon.

I went to the shop first to arrange my affairs, and after explaining the situation to Nadal, he offered to help me. He loved doctoring official paperwork, he said. It reminded him of his finest working days. We made a copy of the original certificate and then corrected it so that the name was mine. We changed the address, the birth date, and typed the particulars of my height and weight on a beat-up Underwood Nadal had inherited from his days in customs. He whistled the whole time, clearly enjoying himself. "You've made an old man feel young again," he said. We reprinted the form on bond paper, and with great ceremony, Nadal brought out a dusty box from beneath his desk. In it were the official stamps he'd pilfered over the years, more than a dozen of them, including one from the OFFICE OF THE SECRETARY GENERAL OF THE PATRIOTIC FORCES OF NATIONAL DEFENSE—that is, from the dictator himself. It had a mother-of-pearl handle and an intricate and stylized version of the national seal. I'd never seen anything like it. A keepsake, Nadal told me, from an affair with an unscrupulous woman who covered him, twice weekly, in bite marks and lurid scratches, and who screamed so loudly when they made love that he often stopped just to marvel at the sound. "Like a banshee," he said. She maintained similar liaisons with the dictator, and according to the woman, he liked to decorate her naked body with this same stamp. Nadal smiled. He could reasonably claim to have been, in his prime, extraordinarily close to the seat of power.

"Of course, the king is dead," Nadal said. "And me, I'm still alive."

Each stamp had a story like this, and he relished the telling—where it had come from, what agency it represented, how it had been used and abused over the years and to what ends. Though Malena was waiting for me, we spent nearly two hours selecting a stamp, and then we placed the forged document, and the target that I'd removed from my wall that morning, in a manila envelope. This too was sealed with a stamp.

Nadal and I embraced. "There'll always be a job for you here," he said.

Malena and I rode home that day on a groaning interprovincial bus. She fell asleep with her head on my shoulder, and when I saw the city disappear and give way to the rolling plains and gentle contours of the countryside, I was not unhappy. The next morning I presented the documents at the bank in the town just across the bridge from mine. "We've been needing a security guard," the manager said. "You may have heard what happened to our last one." He blinked a lot as he spoke. "You're young, but I like the looks of you. I don't know why, but I like the looks of you." And then we shook hands; I was home again.

MY SON WAS BORN just before Christmas that year, and in March the papers began reporting a string of bank robberies in the provinces. The perpetrators were ex-convicts, or foreigners, or soldiers thrown out of work since the democratic government began downsizing the army. No one knew for certain, but it was worrisome and new, as these were the sorts of crimes that had been largely confined to the city and its poorer suburbs. Everyone was afraid, most of all me. Each report was grislier than the last. A half hour upriver, two clerks had been executed after the contents of the vault had disappointed the band of criminals. They hit two banks that day, shooting their way through a police perimeter at the second one, killing one cop and wounding another in the process. They were said to be traveling the river's tributaries, hiding in coves along the heavily forested banks. Of course, it was only a matter of time. The bank I worked for received sizable deposits from the cement plant once a week, and many of the workers cashed their checks with us on alternate Friday afternoons.

Malena read the papers, heard the rumors, and catalogued the increasingly violent details of each heist. I heard her tell her friends she wasn't worried, that I was a sure shot, but in private, she was unequivocal. "Quit," she said. "We have a son to raise. We can move back to the city."

But something had changed. The three of us were living together in the same room where I'd grown up. She smothered our son with so much affection that I barely felt he was mine at all. The boy was always hungry, and I woke every predawn when he cried, and watched as he fed with an urgency I could understand and recall perfectly: it was how I'd felt when I left for the city almost exactly a year before. Afterward, I could never get back to sleep, and I wondered how and when I'd become so hopelessly, so irredeemably selfish, and what, if anything, could be done about it. None of my actions belonged to me. I'd been living one kind of life when a strong, implacable hand had pulled me violently into another. I tried to remember my city routines, but I couldn't.

The rest of the world had never seemed so distant.

By late summer the gang hit most of the towns in our province. It was then my father suggested we go out to the old farm. He would teach me how to use the pistol. I began to tell him I knew, but he wasn't interested.

"You'll drive," he said.

We left town on a Saturday of endless, oppressive heat, the road nothing but a sticky band of tar humming beneath us. We arrived just before noon. There were no shadows. The rutted gravel road led right up to the house, shuttered and old and caving in on itself like a ruined cake. My father got out and leaned against the hood of the car. Behind us, a low cloud of dust snaked back to the main road, and a light breeze brushed over the grassy, overgrown fields, but provided no relief. He took out a bottle of rum, drank a little, and pulled the brim of his cap down over his eyes. The light was fierce. He was seven years old when my grandfather died and my grandmother moved the family from this farm into town. He passed me the bottle; I handed him the weapon. He loaded it with a smile, and without saying much, we took turns firing rounds at the sagging walls of my grandfather's house.

An hour passed this way, blowing out what remained of the windows, and circling the house clockwise to try our onslaught from another angle. We aimed for the cornices just below the roof, and hit, after a few attempts, the tilting weather vane above so that it spun maniacally in the still afternoon heat. We shot the numbers off the front door and tore the rain gutter from the corner it had clung to for five decades. I spread holes all over the façade of the tired house. My father watched, and I imagined he was proud of me.

"How does it feel?" he asked when we were finished. We sat leaning against the shadowed eastern wall.

The gun was warm in my hand. "I don't know," I said. "You tell me."

He took his cap off, and laid it by his side. "You're no good with that pistol. You've got to shoot like you mean it."

"I don't."

"It's all right to be scared."

"I know," I said. "I am."

"Your generation isn't lucky. This never would have happened before. The old government wouldn't have allowed it."

I shrugged. I had a postcard of the dead general buried in a bag back home. I could show it to my father anytime, at any moment, just to make him angry or sad or both, and somehow, knowing this felt good.

"Are you enjoying it?" he asked. "Are you enjoying being a father?"

"What kind of question is that?"

"It's not a *kind* of question. It *is* a question. If you're going to take everything your father says as an insult, your life will be unbearable—"

"I'm sorry."

He sighed. "If it isn't already."

We sat, watching the heat rise from the baking earth. It seemed strange to have to deny this to my father—that my life was unbearable. I mentioned the bridge, its new color, but he hadn't noticed.

He turned to face me. "You know, your mother and I are still young."

"Sure you are."

"Young enough, in good health, and I've got years of work left in me." He flexed his bicep, and held it out for me to see. "Look," he said. "Touch if you want. Your old man is still strong."

He was speaking very deliberately now, and I had the feeling that he'd prepared the exact wording of what he said next. "We're young, but you're very young. You have an entire life to lead. And you can go, if you want, and look for that life elsewhere. Go do things, go see different places. We can take care of the child. You don't want to be here, and we understand."

"What are you talking about?"

"Your mother agrees," he said. "We've discussed it. She'll miss you, but she says she understands."

I stared at him. "And Malena?"

"She'll want for nothing."

I picked up the gun, brushed the dust off it. I checked to make sure it was unloaded and passed it back to him.

"When?" I asked.

"Whenever."

And then we rode home and spoke only of the weather and the elections. My father didn't care much for voting, but he supposed if the owner of the plant wanted to be mayor, he could be. It was fine with him. It was all fine with him. The sky had filled with quilted, white clouds, but the heat had not waned. Or maybe it was how I felt. Even with the windows down, I sweated clean through my shirt, my back and thighs sticking fast to the seat. I didn't add much to the conversation, only drove and stared ahead and thought about what my father had said to me. I was still thinking about it two weeks later when we were robbed.

It was no better or worse than I'd imagined. I was asked to say something at the manager's wake, and to my surprise, the words would not come easily. I stood before a room of grieving family and shell-shocked friends, offering a bland remembrance of the dead man and his kindness. I found it impossible to make eye contact with anyone. Malena cradled our son in her arms, and the evening passed in a blur, until the three of us made our way to the corner of the dark parlor where the young widow was receiving condolences. She thanked me for my words; she cooed at our boy. "How old?" she asked, but before Malena or I could respond, her face reddened and the tears came and there was nothing either of us could say. I excused myself, left Malena with a kiss, and escaped through a back door. It was a warm evening, the town shuttered and quiet. I could hardly breathe. I never made it home that night, and of course, this time Malena knew better than to look for me.

ABRAHAM LINCOLN
HAS BEEN SHOT

WE WERE TALKING, Hank and I, about how that which we love is so often destroyed by the very act of our loving it. The bar was dark, but comfortably so, and by the flittering light of the television I could make out the rough texture of his face. He was, in spite of everything, a beautiful man.

We'd lost our jobs at the call center that day, both of us, but Hank didn't seem to care. All day strangers yelled at us, demanding we make their lost packages reappear. Hank kept a handle of bourbon in the break room, hidden behind the coffee filters, for those days when a snowstorm back East slowed deliveries and we were made to answer for the weather. After we were told the news of the firing, Hank spent the afternoon drinking liquor from a styrofoam cup and wandering the floor, mumbling to himself. For one unpleasant hour he stood on two stacked boxes of paper, peering out the high window at the cars baking in the parking lot. I cleaned out my desk, and then his. Things between us hadn't been good in many months.

Hank said: "Take, as an example, Abraham Lincoln."

"Why bring this up?" I asked. "Why tonight?"

"Now, by the time of his death," he said, ignoring me, "Lincoln was the most beloved man in America."

I raised an eyebrow. "Or was he the most hated?"

Hank nodded. "People hated him, yeah. Sure they did. But they also loved him. They'd loved him down to a fine sheen. Like a stone polished by the touch of a thousand hands."

Lincoln was my first love and Hank knew the whole story. He brought it up whenever he wanted to hurt me.

Lincoln and I had met at a party in Chicago, long before he was president, at one of those Wicker Park affairs with fixed-gear bikes locked out front, four deep, to a stop sign. We were young. It was summer. "I'm going to run for president," he said, and all night he followed me—from the spiked punch bowl to the balcony full of smokers to the dingy bedroom where we groped on a stranger's bed. The whole night he never stopped repeating it.

Finally, I gave in: "I'll vote for you."

Lincoln said he liked the idea: me, alone, behind a curtain, thinking of him.

"I don't understand what you mean," I said to Hank.

"Here you are with me. Together, we're a mess. And now the wheels have come off, Manuel."

"Like Lincoln?"

"Everything he did for this nation," Hank said. "The Americans had no choice but to kill him."

I felt a flutter in my chest. "Don't say that," I managed.

Hank apologized. He was always apologizing. He polished off his drink with a flourish, held it up, and shook it. Suddenly he was a bandleader and it was a maraca: the ice rattled wonderfully. A waitress appeared.

"Gimme what I want, sugar," Hank said.

She was chewing gum laconically, something in her posture indicating a painful awareness that this night would be a long one. "How do I know what you want?"

Hank covered his eyes with his hands. "Because I'm famous."

She took his glass and walked away. Hank winked at me and I tried to smile. I wished he could have read my mind. That night it would have made many things between us much simpler.

"The thing is," Hank said once he had a fresh drink, "there's a point after which you have finished loving something, after you have extracted everything of beauty from it, and you must—it is law—discard it."

This was all I could take. "Oh Christ. Just say it."

There was a blinking neon sign behind the bar, and Hank looked over my shoulder, lost himself in its lights. "Say what?" he asked.

"What you want to say."

"I don't know what I want." He crossed his arms. "I never have. I resent the pressure to decide."

Lincoln was a good man, a competent lover, a dignified leader with a tender heart. He'd wanted to be a poet, but settled for being a statesman. "It's just my day job," he told me once. He was sitting naked in a chair in my room when he said it, smoking a cigarette and cleaning the dust from his top hat with a wooden toothbrush. And he was fragile: his ribs showed even then. We were together almost a year. In the mornings, I would comb out his beard for him, softly, always softly, and Lincoln would purr like a cat.

Hank laid his hands flat on the table and studied them. They were veiny and worn. "I'm sorry," he said, without looking up. "It wasn't a good job, was it?"

"No," I said. "But it was a job."

He rubbed his eyes. "If I don't stop drinking, I'm going to be sick. On the other hand, if I stop drinking . . . Oh, this life of ours."

I raised one of Hank's hands and kissed it.

I was a southern boy, and of course it was something Lincoln and I talked about. Hank didn't care where I was from. Geography is an accident, he said. The place you are born is simply the first place you flee. And then: the people you meet, the ones you fall for, and the paths you make together, the entirety of one's life, a series of mere accidents. And these too are accidents: the creeks you stumble upon in a dense wood, the stones you gather, the number of times each skips across the bright surface of the water, and everything you feel in that moment: the graceless passage of time, the possibility of stillness. Lincoln and I had lived this—skipped rocks and felt our hearts swelling—just before he left Illinois for Washington. We were an hour outside Chicago, in a forest being encroached upon by subdivisions. Everywhere we walked that day there were trees adorned with bright orange flags: trees with death certificates, land marked for clearing, to be crisscrossed by roads and driveways, dotted with the homes of upright American yeomen.

Lincoln told me he loved me.

"I'll come with you," I said. I was hopeful. This was years ago.

That morning he'd gone to the asylum to select a wife. The doctors had wheeled her out in a white gown and married them on the spot. Under the right care, they said, she'll make a great companion. Her name was Mary Todd. "She's very handsome," Lincoln said. He showed me a photograph and I admitted that she was.

"Do you love her?" I asked.

Lincoln wouldn't look me in the eye.

"But you just met her today."

He answered with a sigh. When he had been quiet long enough, he took my hand. We had come to a place where the underbrush was so overgrown that the construction markers seemed to get lost: mossy, rotting tree trunks were everywhere, gnarled limbs and tangled vines hung over the trail. Lincoln kept hitting his head as we walked.

"This forest is so messy," he complained.

I said, "You're too fastidious to be a poet."

He gave me a sheepish smile.

Back at the bar, Hank was falling apart before my eyes. Or pretending to. "What will we do?" he pleaded. "How will we pay the rent?"

It was a good question. He slumped his shoulders and I smiled at him. "You don't love me," I said.

He froze for a moment. "Of course I do. Am I not destroying you, bit by bit?"

"Are you?"

Hank's face was red. "Wasn't it me that made you lose your job?"

It was good to hear him say it. Hank had been in the habit of transferring his most troublesome callers to me, but not before thoroughly antagonizing them, not before promising that their lost package was only the beginning, that they could expect far worse, further and more violent attacks on their suburban tranquility. Inevitably they demanded to speak to a manager, and I would be forced to bail out my lover. Or try to. I wasn't a manager, I never had been, and the playacting was unbearable. The customer barked insults and I gave it all away: shipping, replacements, insurance, credit, anything to get them off the line. Hank would be listening in from his cubicle, breathing a little too heavily into the receiver, and I knew I was disappointing him. Afterward, he would apologize tearfully, and two weeks might pass, maybe three, before it would happen again.

It took Accounting months to pin it on us.

Now Hank sighed. "What would you have done without me anyway? How could you have survived that place?"

I didn't answer him.

We emptied our pockets, left the bar, and walked into the night. The heat outside was never-ending. It was eleven-thirty or later, and still the desert air was dense. This time of year, those of us who were not native, those whom life had ship-wrecked in the great Southwest, began to confront a very real terror: summer was coming. Soon it would be July and there would be no hope. We made our way to the truck. Hank tossed me the keys and I caught them, just barely. It was the first good thing that had happened all day. If they'd hit the ground, we surely would've spent hours on hands and knees, palming the warm desert asphalt, looking for them.

"Where to?" I asked.

"You know."

I drove slowly through downtown, and then under the Ninth Avenue Bridge, and into the vast anonymity of tract homes and dry gullies, of evenly spaced streetlights with nothing to illuminate. We had friends who lived around here, grown women who collected crystals and whose neighborhood so depressed them that they often got in the car just to find somewhere else to walk the dog. Still, beneath the development, it was beautiful country: after a half hour, the road smoothed out; another ten minutes and the lights vanished, and then you could really move. With the windows down and the hot air rushing in, you could pretend it was a nice place to live. A few motor homes tilting on cinder blocks, an abandoned shopping cart in a ditch, glittering in the headlights like a small silver cage—and then it was just desert, which is to say there was nothing at all but dust and red rock and an indigo sky speckled with stars. Hank had his hand on my knee, but I was looking straight ahead, to that point just beyond the reach of the headlights. With an odd job or two, we might be able to scrounge together rent. After that, it was anyone's guess and the very thought was exhausting. I felt— incorrectly, it turns out—that I was too old to have nothing again.

Lincoln and I spent a winter together in Chicago. He was on the city council and I worked at a deli. We couldn't afford heat, and so every night we would curl our bodies together, beneath a half-dozen blankets, and hold tight, skin on skin, until the cold was banished. In the middle of the night, the heat between us would suddenly become so intense that either he or I or the both of us would throw the covers off. It happened every night, and every morning it was a surprise to wake, shivering, with the bedclothes rumpled on the floor.

I'd made my way to southern Florida by the time he was killed. It had been eleven years since we'd been in touch. For the duration of the war I had wandered the country, looking for work. There was a white woman who had known my mother, and when I wrote to her, she offered me a place to stay in exchange for my labor. It seemed fine for a while. At dusk the cicadas made their plaintive music, and every morning we rose before dawn and cleared the undergrowth and dug canals in an endless attempt to drain the land. There were three men besides me, connected by an obscure system of relations stretching back into the region's dim history: how it was settled and conquered, how its spoils had been divided. There was a lonely Cherokee and a Carib who barely spoke and a freed black who worked harder than the three of us together. The white woman had known all of our mothers, had watched us grow up and scatter and return. She intended to plant orange trees, just as she'd seen in a brochure once on a trip to Miami: trees in neat little rows, the dull beauty of progress.

But this land was a knot, just a dense, spongy mangrove atop a bog. You could cup the dirt in your hands, squeeze it, and get water. "It'll never work," I said one afternoon, after a midday rain shower had undone in forty-five minutes what we had spent a week building. She fired me then and there, no discussion, no preamble. "Men should be more optimistic," she said, and gave me a half hour to gather my things.

It was the freed black who drove me to the bus station. When he had pulled the old truck out onto the road, he took his necklace from beneath his shirt. There was a tiny leather pouch tied to it.

"What is it?" I asked.

"It's a bullet." He turned very serious. "And there's a gun hidden in the glade."

"Oh," I said.

He barely opened his mouth when he spoke. "That woman owned my mother, boy, and that land is going to be mine. Do you understand me now? Do you get why I work so hard?"

I nodded, and suddenly felt a respect for him, for the implacability of his will, that was nearly overwhelming. When I had convinced him I understood, he turned on the radio, and that's when we heard the news: Ford's Theatre, the shooting, *Sic semper tyrannis*. The announcer faded in and out; and though I would miss my bus because of it, we found a place with good reception and, without having to say a word, both agreed to stop. The radio prattled breathlessly—the assassin had escaped—no, they had caught him—no, he had escaped.

It was a wretched country we were living in, stinking, violent, diseased. I listened, not understanding, and didn't notice for many minutes that my companion had shut his eyes and begun, very quietly, to weep. He closed his right fist around the bullet, and with the other gripped the steering wheel, as if to steady himself.

I've been moving west since.

That night we were fired, Hank and I made it to the highway, heading south, and then everything was easy. Along the way I forgot where we were going, and then remembered, and then forgot again. I decided it was better not to remember, that something would present itself, and so when the front right tire blew, it was like I'd been waiting for it all night. Hank had dozed, and now the truck shook violently, with a terrific noise, but somehow I negotiated it—me and the machine and the empty night highway—in that split second, a kind of ballet. Hank came to when we had eased onto the shoulder. I was shaking, but alive.

"What did you do?" he asked, blinking. "Is this Mexico?"

It seemed very real, what I felt: that truck had, through mechanical intuition, decided to blow a tire for me, to force me to stop. I turned on the cabin light. "How long has it been since you stopped loving me?"

"Really?" he asked.

I nodded.

"What month is this?" Hank said desperately.

I didn't budge.

"Are you going to leave me here?"

"Yes," I said.

He smiled, as if this were a moment for smiling. "I'm not getting out. I paid for this truck."

"No you didn't," I said.

"Still," he shrugged, "I'm not getting out."

Which was fine. Which was perfect. There was a spare in the back, but it was flat too. If one must begin again late in life, better to do so cleanly, nakedly. I left the keys in the ignition. Out here, outside our small city, the air had cooled and I breathed it in. Life is very long. It had been years, but I recognized the feeling immediately. It wasn't the first time I'd found myself on a dark highway, on foot, with nowhere to go.

THE PROVINCIALS

I'D BEEN OUT OF THE CONSERVATORY for about a year
when my great-uncle Raúl died. We missed the funeral, but
my father asked me to drive down the coast with him a few
days later, to attend to some of the postmortem details. The
house had to be closed up, signed over to a cousin. There were
a few boxes to sift through as well, but no inheritance or anything like that.

I was working at the copy shop in the Old City, trying
out for various plays, but my life was such that it wasn't hard to
drop everything and go. Rocío wanted to come along, but I
thought it'd be nice for me and my old man to travel together.
We hadn't done that in a while. We left the following morning, a Thursday. A few hours south of the capital, the painted
slums thinned, and our conversation did too, and we took in
the desolate landscape with appreciative silence. Everything
was dry: the silt-covered road, the dirty white sand dunes,

somehow even the ocean. Every few kilometers, there rose out of this moonscape a billboard for soda or beer or suntan lotion, its colors faded since the previous summer, its edges un-glued and flapping in the wind. This was years ago, before the beaches were transformed into private residences for the wealthy, before the ocean was fenced off and the highway pushed back, away from the land's edge. Back then, the coast survived in a state of neglect, and one might pass the occasional fishing village, or a filling station, or a rusting pyramid of oil drums stacked by the side of the road, a hitchhiker, perhaps a laborer, or a woman and her child strolling along the highway with no clear destination. But mostly you passed nothing at all. The monotonous landscape gave you a sense of peace, all the more because it came so soon after the city had ended.

We stopped for lunch at a beach town four hours south of the capital, just a couple dozen houses built on either side of the highway, with a single restaurant serving only fried fish and soda. There was absolutely nothing remarkable about the place, except that after lunch we happened upon the last act of a public feud: two local men, who might've been brothers or cousins or best of friends, stood outside the restaurant, hands balled in tight fists, shouting at each other in front of a tipped-over mototaxi. Its front wheel spun slowly, but did not stop. It refused to stop. It was like a perpetual motion machine. The passenger cage was covered with heavy orange plastic, and painted on the side was the word JOSELITO.

And I wondered: *Which of these two men is Joselito?*

The name could've fit either of them. The more aggressive of the pair was short and squat, his face rigid with fury. His reddish eyes had narrowed to tiny slits. He threw wild punches and wasted vast amounts of energy, moving like a spinning top around his antagonist. His rival, both taller and wider, started off with a look of bemused wonder, almost embarrassment, but the longer the little one kept at it, the more his expression darkened, so that within minutes, their moods were equally matched.

Perhaps ownership of this name was precisely what they were arguing about, I thought. The wheel clicked at every rotation, and though I knew it was impossible, I was certain it was getting louder each time. The longer that front wheel kept spinning, the more disconcerted I became. The combatants danced around each other, now lunging, now retreating, both deeply committed to resolving the issue—whatever it might be—right then, right there.

A boy of about eighteen stood next to my father and me. With crossed arms, he observed the proceedings as if it were a horse race on which he'd wagered a very small sum. He wore no shoes, and his feet were dusted with sand. Though it wasn't particularly warm, he'd been swimming. I ventured a question.

"Which one is Joselito?" I asked.

He looked at me like I was crazy. He had a fuzzy blue

name tattooed on his forearm, blurred and impossible to read. His girlfriend's name? His mother's?

"Don't you know?" he said in a low voice. "Joselito's dead."

I nodded, as if I'd known, as if I'd been testing him, but by then the name of the dead man was buzzing around the gathered circle of spectators, whispered from one man to the next, to a child, then to his mother, so that it seemed, for a moment, that the entire town was humming it: "Joselito, Joselito."

A chanting; a conjuring.

The two rivals continued, more furiously now. The mention of the dead man had animated them, or freed some brutal impulse within them. The smaller one landed a right hook to the bigger man's jaw, and this man staggered, but did not fall. The crowd *ooh*ed and *aah*ed, and it was only then that the two fighters realized they were being watched. I mean, they'd known it all along, of course; they must have. But when the crowd reached a certain mass, the whispering a certain volume, with all these many eyes fixed upon the arguing men—then everything changed. It could not have been more staged if they'd been fighting in an amphitheater, with an orchestra playing behind them. It was something I'd been working out myself, in my own craft: how the audience affects a performance, how differently we behave when we know we are being watched. True authenticity, I'd decided, required an absolute, nearly spiritual denial of the audience, or even of the possibility of being watched; but here, something true, something real, quickly morphed into something fake. It happened instantaneously, on a sandy street in this anonymous town: we were no longer accidental observers of an argument, but the primary reason for its existence. This awareness on the part of the protagonists served to alter and magnify their behavior, their gestures, and their expressions of anger. The scene was suddenly more dramatic, their taunts more carefully phrased, more pointed.

"This is for Joselito!" the little man shouted.

"No! *This* is for Joselito!" responded the other.

And so on.

The crowd cheered them both without prejudice. Or perhaps they were cheering the dead man. Whatever the case, soon blood was drawn, lips swollen, eyes blackened. And still the wheel spun. My father and I watched with rising anxiety— someone might die! Why won't that wheel stop!—until, to our relief, a town elder rushed through the crowd and pushed the two men apart. He was frantic. He stood between them, arms spread like wings, a flat palm pressed to each man's chest as they leaned steadily into him.

This too was part of the act.

"Joselito's father," said the barefoot young man. "Just in time."

"Naturally," I said.

We left and drove south for another hour before coming

to a stretch of luxurious new asphalt, so smooth it felt like the car might be able to pilot itself. The tension washed away, and we were happy again, until we found ourselves trapped amid the thickening swarm of trucks headed to the border. We saw northbound traffic being inspected, drivers being shaken down, small-time smugglers dispossessed of their belongings. The soldiers were adolescent and smug, wishing, I assumed, that they'd been stationed somewhere more lucrative. Everyone paid. We would too when it was our turn to head back to the city. This was all new, my father said, and he gripped the wheel tightly and watched with mounting concern. Or was it anger? This corruption, the only kind of commerce that had thrived during the war, was also the only kind we could always count on. Why he found it so disconcerting, I couldn't figure. Nothing could have been more ordinary.

By nightfall we'd made it to my father's hometown. My great-uncle's old filling station stood at the top of the hill, under new ownership and doing brisk business now, though the truckers rarely ventured into the town proper. We eased the car onto the main street, a palm-lined boulevard that sloped down to the boardwalk, and left it a few blocks from the sea, walking until we reached the simple public square that overlooked the ocean. A larger palm tree, its trunk inscribed with the names and dates of young love, stood in the middle of this inelegant plaza. Every summer, the tree was optimistically engraved with new names and new dates, and then stood for the entire winter, untouched. I'd scratched a few names there myself, years before. On warm nights, when the town filled with families on vacation, the children brought out remote-control cars and guided these droning machines around the plaza, ramming them into one another or into the legs of adults, occasionally tipping them off the edge of the boardwalk and onto the beach below, and celebrating these calamities with cheerful hysteria.

My brother, Francisco, and I had spent entire summers like this, until the year he'd left for the U.S. These were some of my favorite memories.

But in the off-season, there was no sign of these young families. No children. They'd all gone north, back to the city or farther, so naturally, the arrival of one of the town's wandering sons was both unexpected and welcome. My father and I moved through the plaza like rock stars, stopping at every bench to pay our respects, and from each of these aged men and women I heard the same thing. First: brief, rote condolences on the death of Raúl (it seems no one much cared for him); then, a smooth transition to the town's most cherished topic of discussion, the past. The talk was directed at me:

"Your old man was so smart, so brilliant . . ."

My father nodded, politely accepting every compliment, not the least bit embarrassed by the attention. He'd carried the town's expectations on his shoulders for so many years they no longer weighed on him. I'd heard these stories all my life.

"This is my son," he'd say. "You remember Nelson?"

And one by one the old folks asked when I had come back from the United States.

"No, no," I said, "I'm the other son."

Of course, they got us confused, or perhaps simply forgot I existed. Their response, offered gently, hopefully: "Oh, yes, the *other* son." Then, leaning forward: "So, when will you be leaving?"

It was late summer, but the vacation season had come to an early close, and already the weather had cooled. In the distance, you could hear the trucks humming along the highway. The bent men and stooped women wore light jackets and shawls, and seemed not to notice the sound. It was as if they'd all taken the same cocktail of sedatives, content to cast their eyes toward the sea, the dark night, and stay this way for hours. Now they wanted to know when I'd be leaving.

I wanted to know too.

"Soon," I said.

"Soon," my father repeated.

Even then I had my doubts, but I would keep believing this for another year or so.

"Wonderful," responded the town. "Just great."

My father and I settled in for the night at my great-uncle's house. It had that stuffiness typical of shuttered spaces, of old people who live alone, made more acute by the damp ocean air. The spongy foam mattresses sagged and there were yellowing photographs everywhere—in dust-covered frames, in unruly stacks, or poking out of the books that lined the shelves of the living room. My father grabbed a handful and took them to the kitchen. He set the water to boil, flipping through them idly and calling out names of the relatives in each picture. There was a flatness to his voice, a distance—as if he were testing his recall, as opposed to reliving any cherished childhood memory. You got the sense he barely knew these people.

He handed me a small black-and-white image with a matte finish, printed on heavy cardstock with scalloped edges. It was a group shot taken in front of this very house, back when it was surrounded by fallow land, the bare, undeveloped hillside. Perhaps twenty blurred faces.

"Besides a few of the babies," my father said, "everyone else in this photo is dead."

For a while we didn't speak.

A bloom of mold grew wild on that kitchen wall, bursting black and menacing from a crack in the concrete. To pass the time, or change the subject, we considered the mold's shape, evocative of something, but we couldn't say what. A baby carriage? A bull?

No, it was something else.

"Joselito's mototaxi," my father said.

And this was, in fact, exactly what it resembled.

"May he rest in peace," I added.

Poor Joselito. His mototaxi somehow imprinted on the wall in mold, transformed into a blackish-green blob; the only detail missing was the spinning wheel. We'd left the town without learning a thing about him—not how he died, not how old he was, not whom he'd left behind. The fight had ended shortly after the town elder stepped between the antagonists; ended, in fact, with a generalized sigh, then a cheer, which somehow became a dirge, and then suddenly, all around us, everyone wept openly for the dead man. The town elder too, who'd seemed only a moment before so determined and fierce and imperturbable, now strained to hold back tears, biting his lip, shaking from the effort to keep his emotions under control. I noticed the wheel had finally stopped. The fighters embraced, and then everyone did, except my father, who stood apart from it all. I tried to pull him in, but he shrugged me off, and then the barefoot, tattooed boy took my hand and dragged me to the center of this lachrymose circle of strangers. I didn't cry, but I wasn't *opposed* to it. Only the tears wouldn't come.

My father had been quiet for most of the trip—coming home always did this to him—but he spoke up now. Joselito, he said, must have been a real character. Someone special. He hadn't seen an outpouring of emotion like that in many years, not since he was a boy.

"It was an act," I said, and began to explain my theory.

My old man interrupted me. "But what isn't?"

What he meant was, people perform sorrow for a reason. For example: no one in this town was performing it for Raúl. My great-uncle had been mayor of this town when my father was a boy, had owned the filling station, and sired seven children with five different women, none of whom he bothered to marry. He'd run the town's only radio station for a decade, and paid from his own pocket to pave the main boulevard so he could drive in style. Then in the late 1980s, he lost most of his money, and settled into a bitter seclusion. I remembered him only for his bulbous nose, and his hatred of foreigners, an expansive category in which he placed anyone who wasn't originally from the town and its surrounding areas. Raúl's distrust of the capital was absolute. I was eleven the last time I saw him, and I don't think he ever trusted me.

It was easier to talk about Joselito than about my great-uncle. More pleasant perhaps. This town brought up bad memories for my father, who was, in those days, entering a pensive late middle age. That was how it seemed to me at the time; but what does a twenty-two-year-old know about a grown man's life and worries? Very little, of course. I was too young to recognize what would later seem more than obvious: that I was the greatest source of my old man's concern. That, if he was growing old too soon, I was at least partly to blame. This would've been clear had I been paying attention. We hadn't come to see about Raúl or his house or his things. We'd come to see about me.

My father shifted the conversation in that direction. He asked me what I planned to do when I got to California. This was typical of the time, a speculative game we were fond of playing. We assumed it was fast approaching, the date of my departure; later I would think we'd all been pretending.

"I don't know," I said.

I'd spent so much time imagining it—my leaving, my preparations, my victory lap around the city, saying goodbye and good luck to all those who'd be staying behind—but what came after contained few specifics. I'd get off the plane, and then . . . Francisco, I guess, would be there. He'd drive me across the Bay Bridge to Oakland, and introduce me to his life there, whatever that might be. From time to time, when curiosity seized me, I searched for this place online and found news items that helped me begin to envision it: shootings mostly, but also minor political scandals involving graft or misused patronage or a city official with liens on his property; occasionally something really exciting, like an oil tanker lost in fog and hitting a bridge, or the firebombing of a liquor store by one street gang or another. There'd even been a minor riot not too long before, with the requisite smashed windows, a dumpster in flames, and a set of multiracial anarchists wearing bandannas across their faces so that all you could see in the photos were their alert and feral eyes; and I'd wondered then how my brother had chosen to live in a city whose ambience so closely mimicked our own. Could it really be an accident of geography? Or was it some latent homing instinct?

What it all had to do with me was never quite clear. Where I would fit in. What I would do with myself once I was there. These were among the many questions that remained. The visa, whenever it came, would not arrive with life instructions. Nor would it obligate me to stay in Oakland, of course, and I had considered other alternatives, though none very seriously and all based on a whimsical set of readings and the occasional Internet search: Philadelphia I liked for its history; Miami for its tropical ennui; Chicago for its poets; Los Angeles for its sheer size.

But one can start over in any number of places, right? Any number of times?

"I'll get a job," I told my father. "Isn't that what Americans do?"

"It's what everyone does. In a copy shop?"

"I'm an actor."

"Who makes photocopies."

I frowned. "So I'll make photocopies my entire life. Why not?"

He wanted me to study, because that was what he'd wanted for himself so many years before. And for Francisco too. He'd hoped my brother would be a professor by now, an academic, though he was far too proud to ever share this disappointment with me. He had his own issues with me:

his unbounded respect for playwrights and artists and writers was completely abstract—on a more concrete level, he wished I'd considered some more reliable way to earn a living. As for my day job, my mother told me once that seeing me work as the attendant at the copy shop made my old man sad. His unexpressed sadness, in turn, made me angry. His politics affirmed that all work held an inherent dignity. This was what he'd always repeated, but of course no ideology can protect a son from the unwelcome inheritance of his father's ambitions.

"When I was a boy," my father said, "this town was the middle of nowhere. It still is, I know. But imagine it before they rerouted the highway. We knew there was something else out there—another country to the south, the capital to the north—but it felt very far away."

"It was."

"You're right. It was. We were hours from civilization. Six or seven to the border, if not more. But the roads were awful. And *spiritually*—it was even farther. It required a certain kind of imagination to see it."

I smiled. I thought I was making him laugh, but really I was just trying to close off the conversation, shut it down before it headed somewhere I didn't want it to go: "I've always been very imaginative," I said.

My old man knew what I was doing, even if I didn't.

"Yes, son. You have. Maybe not imaginative enough, though."

I didn't want to ask him what he meant, so I sat, letting it linger until the silence forced him to answer my unspoken question.

"I'm sorry," my father said. "I wonder if you've thought much about your future, that's all.

"Sure I have. All the time."

"To the exclusion of thinking about your present?"

"I wouldn't say that."

"What would you say?"

I paused, attempting to strip my voice of any anger before I spoke: "I've thought a great deal about my future, so that my present could seem more livable."

He nodded slowly. The cups steamed, and we sipped our tea carefully. For once, I was grateful for my old man's obsession with tea—it allowed us to pause, gather our thoughts. It excused us from having to talk, and the danger of saying things we might not mean.

"You and Rocío seem well."

I never spoke about my relationships with my parents. They'd only met Rocío a few times.

"Sure. We're doing fine."

There was something else he wanted to ask me, but he didn't. He was wondering how to phrase his concern. He narrowed his eyes, thinking, and then something changed in his face—a slackness emerged, the edges of his mouth dropped. He'd given up.

"I always hated this house," my old man said after a few minutes. "I can't imagine that anyone would want it. We should bulldoze the thing and be done with it."

It was all the same to me, and I told him so. We could set it on fire, or shatter every last brick with a sledgehammer. I had no attachments to this place, to this town. My father did, but he preferred not to think about them. It was a place to visit with a heavy heart, when an old relative died. Or with your family on holiday, if such a luxury could be afforded. Francisco, it occurred to me, might feel the same way toward the city where we'd been raised.

"I've let you down," my old man said. His voice was timid, hushed, as if he hadn't wanted me to hear.

"Don't say that."

"We should have pushed you harder, sent you away sooner. Now . . ." He didn't finish, but I understood that *now*, in his estimation, was far too late.

"It's fine."

"I know it is. Everyone's fine. I'm fine, you're fine, your mother's fine too. Even Francisco is fine, or so the rumor goes, God bless the USA. Everything is fine. Just ask the mummies sitting on the benches out there. They spend every evening telling the same five stories again and again, but if you ask them, they'll respond with a single voice that everything is *just fine*. What do we have to complain about?"

"I'm not complaining," I said.

"I know you aren't. That's precisely what concerns me."

I slumped, feeling deflated. "I'll leave when the visa comes. I can't leave before that. I can't do anything before that."

My father winced. "But it isn't entirely accurate to say you can't do *anything*, is it?"

"I suppose not."

"Consider this: What if it doesn't come? Or what if it comes at an inconvenient time. Let's say you're in love with Rocío—"

"Let's suppose."

"And she doesn't want to leave. So then you stay. What will you do then?"

He was really asking: *What are you doing right now?*

When I didn't say anything, he pressed further, his voice rising in pitch: "Tell me, son. Are you sure you even want that visa? Are you absolutely certain? Do you know yet what you're going to do with your life?"

WE WERE DETERMINED not to shout at each other. Eventually, he went to bed, and I left the house for a walk along the town's perfectly desolate streets, where there was not a car to be seen, nor a person. You could hear the occasional truck roaring by in the distance, but fewer at this hour, like a sporadic wind. It looked like an abandoned stage set, and I wondered: Who's *absolutely certain* about anything? I found a pay phone not far from the plaza, and called Rocío. I wanted her to make me laugh, and I sighed with relief when she answered on the first ring, as if she'd been waiting for my call. Maybe she had. I told her about the drive, about the fight we witnessed, about my great-uncle's dank and oppressive house, filled with pictures of racehorses and marching bands and the various women who'd borne his children and had their hopes and their hearts shattered by this cruel, lonely man. I didn't tell her about the conversation with my father.

"I've taken a lover," Rocío said, interrupting.

It was a game we played; I tried to muster the energy to play along. I didn't want to disappoint her. "And what's he like?"

"Handsome, in an ugly sort of way. Crooked nose, giant cock. More than adequate."

"I'm dying of jealousy," I said. "Literally dying. The life seeps from my tired body."

"Did you know that by law, if a man finds his wife sleeping with another man on their marriage bed, he's allowed to murder them both?"

"I hadn't heard that. But what if he finds them on the couch?"

"Then he can't kill them. Legally speaking."

"So did you sleep with him on our bed?"

"Yes," Rocío answered. "Many, many times."

"And was his name Joselito?"

There was quiet. "Yes. That was his name."

"I've already had him killed."

"But I just saw him this morning."

"He's gone, baby. Say goodbye."

"Goodbye," she whispered.

I was satisfied with myself. She asked me about the town, and I told her that everyone confused me with my brother. So many years separated my family from this place that they'd simply lost track of me. There was room in their heads for only one son; was it any surprise they chose Francisco?

"Oh, that's so sad!" Rocío said. She was mocking me.

"I'm not telling you so you'll feel sorry for me."

"Of course not."

"I'm serious."

"I know," she said, stretching out the word in a way she probably thought was cute, but that just annoyed me.

"I'm hanging up now." The phone card was running out anyway.

"Good night, Joselito," Rocío said, and blew a kiss into the receiver.

WE SPENT A FEW HOURS the next morning in my great-uncle's house, sifting through the clutter, in case there was anything we might want to take back with us. There wasn't. My father set some items aside for the soldiers, should it come to that; nothing very expensive, but things he thought might *look* expensive if you were a bored young man with a rifle who'd missed all the action by a few years, and were serving your time standing by the side of a highway, collecting tribute: a silver picture frame, an antique camera in pristine condition, an old but very ornate trophy that would surely come back to life with a little polish. It didn't make much sense, of course; these young men wanted one of two things, I told my father: cash or electronics. Sex, perhaps, but probably not with us. Anything else was meaningless. My father agreed. We'd have to pay them or outrun them or dress up as women and be abused by them. Charming options all.

Our unfinished conversation was not mentioned.

After lunch, we headed into town. There was some paperwork to be filed in order to transfer Raúl's property over to a distant cousin of ours, an unmarried woman of fifty who still lived nearby, and might have some use for the house. Raúl's children wanted nothing, refused, on principle, to be involved. My father was dreading this transfer, of course; not because he was reluctant to give up the property—he was, in fact, eager to be rid of it—but because he was afraid of how many hours this relatively simple bureaucratic chore might require. But he hadn't taken his local celebrity into account, and of course we were received at city records with the same bright and enthusiastic palaver with which we'd been welcomed in the plaza the night before. We were taken around to greet each of the dozen municipal employees, friendly men and women of my father's generation and older, who welcomed the interruption because they quite clearly had nothing to do. It was just like evenings in the plaza, I thought, only behind desks and under fluorescent lights. Many of them claimed some vague familial connection to me, especially the older ones, and so I began calling them all *uncle* and *auntie* just to be safe. Again and again I was mistaken for Francisco— "When did you get back? Where are you living now?"—and I began to respond with increasingly imprecise answers, so that finally, when we'd made it inside the last office, the registrar of properties, I simply gave in to this assumption, and said, when asked: "I live in California."

It felt good to say it. A relief.

The registrar was a small, very round man named Juan, with dark skin and a raspy voice. He'd been my father's best friend in third grade, or so he claimed. My old man didn't bother to contradict him, only smiled in such a way that I understood it to be untrue; or if not untrue exactly, then one of those statements that time had rendered unverifiable, and about which there was no longer any use debating.

The registrar liked my answer. He loosened his tie and clapped his hands: "California! Oh my! So what do you do there?"

My father gave me a once-over. "Yes," he said now. "Tell my old friend Juan what you do."

I thought back to all those letters my brother had written, all those stories of his I'd read and very nearly memorized in my adolescence. It didn't matter, of course: I could have told Juan any number of things: about my work as a ski instructor, or as a baggage handler, or as a bike-repair technician. I could have told him the ins and outs of Walmart, about life in American small towns, about the shifting customs and mores of different regions of the vast United States. The accents, the landscapes, the winters. Anything I said at that moment would've worked just fine. But I went with something simple and current, guessing correctly that Juan wasn't much interested in details. There were a few facts I knew about my brother, in spite of the years and the distance: a man named Hassan had taken him under his wing. They were in business together, selling baby formula and low-priced denim and vegetables that didn't last more than a day. The details were arcane to me, but it was a government program, which, somehow, was making them both very rich.

"I work with an Arab," I said. "We have a store."

The registrar nodded severely, as if processing this critical information. "The Arabs are very able businessmen," he said finally. "You must learn everything you can from this Arab."

"I intend to."

"So you can be rich!"

"That's the idea," I said.

A smile flashed across Juan's face. "And the American girls? Ehhhhh?"

His voice rose with this last syllable, so that it sounded like the thrum of a small revving motor—that motor being his heart, naturally.

I told him what he wanted to hear, in exactly the sly tone his little motor required: "They're very *affectionate*."

Juan clapped again. "Wonderful! Wonderful! These young people," he said to my father. "The whole world is right there for them, just ripe for the taking. Tell me, are you happy, young man?"

I had to remind myself he was addressing that version of me that lived in California, that worked with Hassan, the one who was going to be unspeakably wealthy as a result. Not the me who'd never left the country, who wanted to be an actor, but was actually a part-time employee in a copy shop run by a depressive.

"Yes," I said. "Yes, I'm very happy."

Juan smiled broadly, and I knew my part in the conversation was over. He and my father got down to business. I sat, trying not to move, as they went over the forms that had to be filled out, and very soon I felt entirely invisible. I watched this man, scanned his office, looking for some clue about his disappointments, but there was none to be found. In many ways, I guess it was obvious, but still I filed the mystery away with the trip's other unknowables: the death of Joselito, for example, or the content of Francisco's most recent letter. Meanwhile, the paperwork was prepared, a long stack of forms and obtusely worded declarations, all signed in triplicate, and in a matter of minutes, my great-uncle's house was officially no longer our problem. I stood when my father did. Juan took my hand, and shook it vigorously.

"California!" he said again, as if he didn't quite believe it.

Once we were free of Juan and the municipal offices, outside again and breathing the briny, life-giving sea air, I congratulated my old man. I said: "Now we don't have to burn the house down."

He gave me a weary look. "Now we can't, you mean."

We walked toward the plaza. It was late afternoon, still hours of light remaining, but where else could one go in this town? The regulars would be in their habitual spots, waiting for the sunset with steadfast, unflagging patience. It had been barely a day, but already I could see quite clearly why my father had fled this place the moment he had the chance. He'd gone first to the provincial capital, a warm picturesque city of broad avenues and blue skies, where he'd won a scholarship to study; but he soon outgrew that city too, and moved to the capital itself, where he finished his education, won more prizes, was married, and went abroad, fulfilling, if only partially, the expectations of those he'd left behind. And his own. They'd wanted him to be a judge, or a diplomat, or an engineer. To build bridges or make law or become wealthy and famous. His actual job—head librarian of the Antiquarian Books and Rare Manuscripts section of the National Library—was a wholly inconceivable occupation. It sounded less like work one did for a wage, and more like an inherited title of nobility. But then it was precisely the rarefied nature of his position that gave my father such prestige in these parts.

We hadn't gone far when he said, "Quite the act in there."

I was feeling good, and opted not to listen for any trace of sarcasm. Instead I thanked him.

"An Arab?" he said. "A store? How precise!"

"Everything's an act, right? I was improvising. You have to say the lines like you mean them."

"I see your studies at the conservatory have really paid dividends. It was very convincing."

"Your best friend thought so."

"Best friend, indeed," my old man said. "I suppose it's obvious, but I believe I have no memory of him."

I nodded. "I don't think he noticed, if that's what you're worried about."

We still hadn't returned to the discussion of the previous night, and now there seemed no point. Instead we'd come to the plaza, with its view of the sea, and its benches filling up one by one. We ducked into a tiny restaurant, hoping to have a quiet meal alone, but naturally everyone there recognized my father, and so the basic ritual of our stay in town began anew. We entered the dining room, waving, accepting greetings. A few men called my father's name excitedly—Manuel! Manolito!—and by the way his face shifted, the way his eyes darkened, I could see this prominence beginning to weigh on him. I saw him draw a deep breath, as if preparing for a steep climb. He was bored with it all, though every instinct told him he must bury this cynicism, ignore it. There are no cynics in this town—that is something you learn when you travel. When you live in the capital and become corrupt. One cannot be rude to these people; one cannot make fun of them. They know almost nothing about you anymore, but they love you. And this was the bind my old man was in. The night demanded something, some way to shift its course; and perhaps this was why, when we approached the table that had called us, he threw an arm over my shoulder, squeezed me tightly, and introduced me as his son Nelson, home from abroad.

"From California," my father said. "Just back for a visit."

I suppose it shouldn't have, but his announcement caught me by surprise. I hadn't intended to reprise the role debuted in Juan's office, but now there was no choice. I scarcely had a moment to glance in my old man's direction, to catch sight of his playful smile, before a couple of strangers wrapped me in a welcoming embrace. Everything happened quite quickly. A few narrow wooden tables were pushed together; my father and I pressed into perversely straight-backed chairs. We were surrounded. Everyone wanted to say hello; everyone wanted to get a look at me. I shook what seemed like a dozen hands, grinning the entire time like a politician. I felt very grateful to my old man for this opportunity. It was—how do I explain this?—the role I'd been preparing for my entire life.

[Scene: A dim restaurant off the plaza, in a small town on the southern coast. Santos (fifteen or twenty years older than the others, whom they call Profe) and his protégé, Cochocho, do most of the talking; Erick and Jaime function as a chorus, and spend most of their energy drinking. They've been at it all afternoon when an old friend, Manuel, arrives with his son Nelson. It is perhaps two hours before dark. Manuel lives in the capital, and his son is visiting from the United States. The young man is charming, but arrogant, just as they expect all Americans to be. As the night progresses, he begins to grate on them, something evident at first only in small gestures. Bottles of beer are brought to the table, the empties are taken away, a process as fluid and automatic as the waves along the beach. How they are drained so quickly is not entirely clear. It defies any law of physics. The waitress, Elena, is an old friend too, a heavyset woman in her late forties, dressed in sweatpants and a loose-fitting T-shirt, who observes these men with a kind of pity. Over the years, she has slept with all of them. A closely guarded secret; they are men of ordinary

vanity, and each of the four locals thinks he is the only one. Elena's brown-haired daughter, Celia, is a little younger than the American boy—he's in his early twenties—and she lingers in the background, trying to catch a glimpse of the foreigner. Her curiosity is palpable. There are dusty soccer trophies above the bar, and a muted television, which no one watches. Occasionally the on-screen image lines up with the dialogue, but the actors are not aware of this.]

NELSON: That's right. California. The Golden State.

ERICK: Hollywood. Sunset Boulevard.

COCHOCHO: Many Mexicans, no?

ERICK: Route 66. James Dean.

JAIME: I have a nephew in Las Vegas. Is that California?

COCHOCHO: *[after opening a bottle of beer with his teeth]* Don't answer him. He's lying. He doesn't even know where Las Vegas is. He doesn't know where California is. Ignore him. Ignore the both of them. That's what we do.

ERICK: Magic Johnson. The Olympics.

COCHOCHO: *[to Erick]* Are you just saying words at random? Do you ever listen to yourself? *[to Nelson]* Forgive him. Forgive us. It's Friday.

NELSON: Forgiven. Naturally.

JAIME: Friday is an important day.

ERICK: The day before Saturday.

NELSON: Of course.

JAIME: And after Thursday.

COCHOCHO: As I said, forgive us.

SANTOS: *[The oldest of the group, also the most formal in speech and demeanor. Suit and tie. He's been waiting for the right moment to speak. He imagines everyone else has been waiting for this too, for their opportunity to hear him.]* I'm appalled by all this. This . . . What is the phrase? This lack of discipline. We must be kind to our guest. Make a good impression. Is it very loud in here? Perhaps you don't notice it. I'm sure things are different where you live. Orderly. I was your father's history teacher. That is a fact.

[Nelson looks to his father for confirmation. A nod from Manuel.]

MANUEL: He was. And I remember everything you taught me, Profe.

SANTOS: I doubt that. But it was my class, I believe, that inculcated in your father the desire to go north, to the capital. I take responsibility for this. Each year, my best students leave. I'm retired now and I don't miss it. It was sad watching them go. Of course they have their reasons. If these others had been paying any attention at all to history as I taught it, they might have understood the logic of migration. It's woven into the story of this nation. I don't consider this something to celebrate, but they might have understood it as a legacy they'd inherited. They might have been a bit more ambitious.

COCHOCHO: Profe, you're being unfair.

SANTOS: *[to Nelson, ignoring Cochocho]* Your father was the best student I ever had.

MANUEL: *[sheepishly]* Not true, Profe, not true.

SANTOS: Of course it's true. Are you calling me a liar? Not like these clowns. I taught them all. *[nodding toward Erick, who is pouring himself a glass of beer]* This one could barely read. Couldn't sit still. Even now, look at him. Doesn't even know who the president is.

[Television: generic politician, his corruption self-evident, as clear as the red sash across his chest.]

The only news he cares about is the exchange rate.

ERICK: The only news that matters. I have expenses. A son and two daughters.

COCHOCHO: *[to Nelson]* And you can marry either of them. Take one of the girls off his hands, please.

SANTOS: Or the boy. That's allowed over there in America, isn't it?

NELSON: How old are the girls?

COCHOCHO: Old enough.

NELSON: Pretty?

ERICK: Very.

COCHOCHO: *[eyebrows raised, skeptical]* A man doesn't look for beauty in a wife. Rather, he doesn't look *only* for beauty. We can discuss the details later. Right, Erick?

[Erick nods absentmindedly. It's as if he's already lost the thread of the conversation.]

SANTOS: So, young man. What do you do in California?

NELSON: *[glancing first at his father]* I have my own business. I work with an Arab. Together we have a store. It's a bit complicated, actually.

SANTOS: Complicated. How's that? What could be simpler than buying and selling? What sort of merchandise is it? Weapons? Metals? Orphans?

[Television: in quick succession, a handgun, a barrel with a biohazard symbol, a sad-looking child. The child remains on-screen, even after Nelson begins speaking.]

NELSON: We began with baby supplies. Milk. Formula. Diapers. That sort of thing. It was a government program. For poor people.

JAIME: Poor Americans?

NELSON: That's right.

COCHOCHO: Don't be so ignorant. There are poor people there too. You think your idiot cousin in Las Vegas is rich?

JAIME: He's my nephew. He wants to be a boxer.

COCHOCHO: [to Nelson] Go on.

NELSON: This was good for a while, but there is—you may have heard. There have been some problems in California. Budgets, and stuff like that.

SANTOS: [dryly] I can assure you these gentlemen have not heard.

NELSON: So we branched out. We rented the space next door, and then the space next door to that. We sell clothes in both. We do well. They come every first and fifteenth and spend their money all at once.

JAIME: You said they were poor.

NELSON: American poor is . . . *different*.

SANTOS: Naturally.

COCHOCHO: Naturally.

NELSON: We drive down to Los Angeles every three weeks to buy the inventory. Garment district. Koreans. Jews. Filipinos. Businessmen.

SANTOS: Very well. An entrepreneur.

MANUEL: He didn't learn this from me.

SANTOS: You speak Arabic now? Korean? Hebrew? Filipino?

NELSON: No. My partner speaks Spanish.

COCHOCHO: And your English?

MANUEL: My son's English is perfect. Shakespearean.

COCHOCHO: Two stores. And they both sell clothes.

NELSON: We have Mexicans, and we have blacks. Unfortunately, these groups don't get along very well. The Mexicans ignore the blacks, who ignore the Mexicans. The white people ignore everyone, but they don't shop with us and so we don't worry about them. We have a store for each group.

SANTOS: But they—they all live in the same district?

[Television: panning shot of an East Oakland street scene: International Boulevard. Mixed crowds in front of taco trucks, tricked-out cars rolling by very slowly, chrome rims spinning, glinting in the fierce sunlight. Latinas pushing strollers, black boys in long white T-shirts and baggy jeans, which they hold up with one hand gripping the crotch.]

NELSON: They do. And naturally, we don't choose sides.

COCHOCHO: Of course not. You're there to make money. Why would you choose sides?

JAIME: But you live there too? With the blacks? With the Mexicans?

[They look him over, a little disappointed. They'd thought he was more successful. Behind the scene, Elena prepares to bring more beer to the table, but her daughter stops her, takes the bottles and goes herself.]

NELSON: Yes. There are white people too.
CELIA: Excuse me, pardon me.

[Celia has inky black eyes, and wears a version of her mother's outfit—an old T-shirt, sweatpants, sandals. On her mother, this clothing represents a renunciation of sexual possibility. On Celia, it represents quite the opposite.]

NELSON: I'd like to buy a round. *[eagerly, wanting to prove himself—to the men? to Celia?]* If I may.
COCHOCHO: I'm afraid that's not possible. *[Slips Celia a few bills.]* Go on, dear.

[She leaves reluctantly. Lingers for a moment, watching Nelson, until her mother shoos her away. Celia disappears offstage. Meanwhile the conversation continues.]

ERICK: You're the guest. Hospitality is important.
SANTOS: These things matter to us. You think it folk-loric, or charming. We're not offended by the way you look at us. We are accustomed to the "anthropo-

logical gaze" *[this last phrase in air quotes]*. We feel sorry for you because you don't understand. We do things a certain way here. We have traditions. *[to Manuel]* How much does your boy know about us? About our town? Have you taught him our customs?

NELSON: I learned the songs when I was a boy.

MANUEL: But he was raised in the city, of course.

COCHOCHO: What a shame. Last time I went was six years ago, when I ran for Congress. A detestable place. I hope you don't mind my saying that.

MANUEL: Certainly you aren't the only one who holds that opinion.

SANTOS: He wanted very badly to win. He would've happily moved his family there.

JAIME: And your wife, she's from the city?

MANUEL: She is.

COCHOCHO: *[to Nelson]* You're lucky to have left. How long have you been in California?

NELSON: Since I was eighteen.

JAIME: It's a terrible place, but still, you must miss home quite a bit.

NELSON: *[laughing]* No, I wouldn't say that, exactly.

ERICK: The food?

NELSON: Sure.

JAIME: The family?

NELSON: Yes, of course.

MANUEL: I'm flattered.

JAIME: Your friends?

NELSON: *[pausing to think]* Some of them.

ERICK: Times have changed.

SANTOS: No, Erick, times have not changed. The youth are not all that different from before. Take Manuel. Let's ask him. Dear Manuel, pride of this poor, miserable village, tell us: How often do you wake up missing this place where you were born? How often do you think back, and wish you could do it over again, never have left, and stayed here to raise a family?

MANUEL: *[Caught off guard, not understanding if the question is serious or not. On the television: a shot of the plaza by night. Quickly recovering, Manuel decides to take the question as a joke.]*
Every day, Profe, naturally.

[Everyone laughs but Santos.]

SANTOS: I thought as much. Some people like change, they like movement, transition. A man's life is very short and of no consequence. We have a different view of time here. A different way of placing value on things. We find everything you Americans—

NELSON: *We* Americans? But I lived in this country until I was eighteen!

SANTOS: *[talking over him]* Everything you Americans say is very funny. Nothing impresses us unless it lasts five hundred years. We can't even begin to discuss the greatness of a thing until it has survived that long.

[It's not clear whom Santos is addressing. Still, there's a murmur of approval. His eyes close. He's a teacher again, in the classroom. He stands.]

So: this town is great. The ocean is great. The desert and the mountains beyond. There are some ruins in the foothills, which you surely know nothing about. They are undoubtedly, indisputably, great, as are the men who built them, and their culture. Their blood, which is our blood, and even yours, though unfortunately . . . How shall I put it? *Diluted.* Not great: the highway, the border. The United States. Where do you live? What's that place called?

NELSON: Oakland, California.

SANTOS: How old?

NELSON: A hundred years?

SANTOS: Not great. Do you understand?

NELSON: I'm sure I don't. If I may: those five-hundred-year-old ruins, for example. You'll notice I'm using your word, Profe. "Ruins." Am I wrong to question whether they've lasted?

[Television: the ruins.]

SANTOS: *[taking his seat again]* You would have failed my class.

NELSON: What a shame. Like these gentlemen?

SANTOS: Nothing to be proud of. Nothing at all.

NELSON: *[transparently trying to win them over]* I'd be in good company.

ERICK: Cheers.

JAIME: Cheers.

MANUEL: *[reluctantly]* Cheers.

COCHOCHO: *[stern, clearing his throat]* I did not fail that class or any class. It's important you know this. I didn't want to mention it, but I am deputy mayor of this town. I once ran for Congress. I could have this bar shut down tomorrow.

ERICK/JAIME: *[together, alarmed]* You wouldn't!

COCHOCHO: Of course not! Don't be absurd! *[pause]* But I *could*. I am a prominent member of this community.

ERICK: Don't be fooled by his name.

COCHOCHO: It's a nickname! A term of endearment! These two? Their nicknames are vulgar. Unrepeatable. And your father? What was your nickname, Manuel?

MANUEL: I didn't have one.

COCHOCHO: Because no one bothered to give him a
name. He was cold. Distant. Arrogant. He looked
down on us even then. We knew he'd leave and
never come back.

[Manuel shrugs. Cochocho, victorious, smiles arrogantly.]

NELSON: Here he is! He's returned!

SANTOS: How lucky we are. Blessed.

COCHOCHO: Your great-uncle's old filling station? It's
mine now. Almost. I have a minority stake in it. My
boy works there. It'll be his someday.

*[As if reminded of his relative wealth, Cochocho orders
another round. No words, only gestures. Again Celia arrives at the table, bottles in hand, as Elena looks on, re-
signed. This time all the men, including Nelson's father,
ogle the girl. She might be pretty after all. She hovers over
the table, leaning in so that Nelson can admire her. He
does, without shame. Television: a wood-paneled motel
room, a naked couple on the bed. The window is open.
They're fucking.]*

SANTOS: *[to Manuel]* Don't take this the wrong way.
The primary issue. What Cochocho is trying to say,
I think, is that some of us . . . We feel abandoned.
Disrespected. You left us. Now your son is talking
down to us.

NELSON: *[amused]* Am I?

MANUEL: Is he?

SANTOS: We don't deserve this, Manuel. You don't re-member! *[to the group]* He doesn't remember! *[to Nelson]* Your father was our best student in a genera-tion. The brightest, the most promising. His father—your grandfather, God rest his soul—had very little money, but he was well-liked, whereas your great-uncle . . . We tolerated Raúl. For a while he was rich and powerful, but he never gave away a cent. He saw your father had potential, but he wanted him to help run the filling station, to organize his properties, to invest. These were his ambitions. Meanwhile, your father, I believe, wanted to be—

NELSON: A professor of literature. At an American university. We've discussed this.

COCHOCHO: Why not a local one?

[Manuel has no response, is slightly ashamed.]

SANTOS: Pardon me. It's a very conventional ambition for a bookish young man. Decent. Middle of the road. You had politics?

MANUEL: I did. *[pause]* I still do.

SANTOS: A rabble-rouser. An agitator. He made some people here very angry, and the teachers—and I was leader of this concerned group, if I remember correctly—we collected money among us, to send him away. We didn't want to see his talent wasted. Nothing destroys our promising youth more than politics. Did he tell you he won a scholarship? Of course. That's a simpler story. He made his powerful uncle angry, and Raúl refused to pay for his studies. Your grandfather didn't have the money either. We sent him away for his own good. We thought he'd come back and govern us well. We hoped he might learn something useful. Become an engineer. An architect. A captain of industry. *[sadly]* We expected more. We needed more. There's no work here. Jaime, for example. What do you do?

JAIME: Sir?

SANTOS: *[impatiently]* I said, what do you do?

JAIME: I'm unemployed. I was a bricklayer.

SANTOS: Erick?

ERICK: I'm a tailor. *[to Nelson, brightly, with an optimism that does not match the mood of the table]* At your service, young man!

SANTOS: See? He made me this suit. Local cotton. Adequate work. I'm on a fixed income. And then there's Cochocho. He is deputy mayor. You know that now. But did you know this? The money he just spent on our drinks? That is our money. He stole it like he stole the election. He brings his suits from the capital. We don't say anything about it because that would be rude. And he is, in spite of his questionable ethics, our friend.

COCHOCHO: *[appalled]* Profe!

SANTOS: What? What did I say? You're not our friend? Is that what you're alleging?

[Cochocho, dejected, unable or unwilling to defend himself. Erick and Jaime comfort him. Just then, Celia reappears, eyes on Nelson. Television: motel room, naked couple in an acrobatic sexual position, a yogic balancing act for two, a scramble of flesh, such that one can't discern whose legs belong to whom, whose arms, how his and her sexual organs are connecting or even if they are.]

CELIA: Another round, gentlemen?

MANUEL: I insist—

NELSON: If you'll allow me—

SANTOS: *[stopping them both with a wave, glaring at Cochocho]* So, are you our friend or not? Will you spend our money or keep it for yourself? *[to Nelson]* Unfortunately, this too is tradition.

NELSON: Five hundred years?

SANTOS: Much longer than that, boy.

NELSON: Please. I'd consider it an honor to buy a round.

COCHOCHO: *[still angry]* Great idea! Let the foreigner spend his dollars!

[At this, Nelson stands and steps toward the startled Celia. He kisses her on the mouth, brazenly, and as they kiss, he takes money from his own pocket, counts it without looking, pushing the bills between his thumb and forefingers, and places it in her hand. She closes her fist around the money, and it vanishes. The exchange happens quickly, expertly, so that we get the impression he's done this before. It's unclear whether he's paying for the drinks or for the kiss itself, but in either case, Celia doesn't question it. The four local men look on, astounded.]

SANTOS: Imperialism!

COCHOCHO: Opportunism!

JAIME: Money!

ERICK: Sex!

[Manuel stares at his son, but says nothing. Takes a drink. Curtain.]

I SHOULD BE CLEAR about something: it is never the words, but how they are spoken that matters. The intent, the tone.

The farcical script quoted above is only an approximation of what actually occurred that evening, after my father challenged me to play Francisco, or a version of him, for this unsuspecting audience. Many other things were said that I've omitted: oblique insults, charmingly ignorant questions, the occasional reference to one or another invented episode of American history. I improvised, using my brother's letters as a guide, even quoting from them when the situation allowed—the line, for example, about Mexicans ignoring blacks and vice versa. That statement was contained within one of Francisco's early dispatches from Oakland, when he was still eagerly trying to understand the place for himself, and not quite able to process the many things he saw. Hassan was a great help, of course, an astute interpreter of the neighborhood's tense race politics. He had experience. He'd watched the situation develop: years before my brother arrived, Hassan was a young man handing out flyers at the corner of Fruitvale Avenue and Foothill Boulevard. Afraid to look anyone in the eye. Stuttering English. Halting Spanish. *Everyone wants to rob me,* Hassan used to think. He gave away cigarettes to everyone who asked. And he stood there, beneath rain and sun, watching people. This pithy observation about Mexicans and blacks, this hard-earned wisdom, came directly from those first days. Hassan offered it to Francisco when he brought him from the port to East Oakland, and Francisco then scribbled it into a letter because it sounded true, and it was read and then delivered by me years later, as if I'd seen this dynamic myself. In a way, I suppose, I had. This is what actors do.

My most significant dramatic choice was to not defend myself all too vigorously. To not defend Oakland, or the United States. That would have been a violation of character, whereas this role was defined by a basic indifference to what was taking place. They could criticize, impugn, belittle—it was all the same to me, I thought (my character thought). They could say what they wanted to say, and I would applaud them for it; after all, at the end of the day, I (my character) would be heading back to the U.S., and they'd be staying here. I needed to let them know this, without saying it explicitly. That's how Francisco would have done it—never entirely sinking into the moment, always hovering above it. Distant. Untouchable.

Through it all, my old man sat very quietly, deflecting attention even when they began discussing him directly, his choices, the meaning and impact of his long exile. I've hurried through the part where my father's friends expressed, with varying levels of obsequiousness, their admiration, their wonder, their jealousy. I've left it out because it wasn't the truth; it was habit—how you treat the prodigal son when he returns, how you flatter him in order to claim some of his success as your own. But this fades. It is less honest, and less interesting than the rest of what took place that night. The surface: Jaime and Erick drank, oblivious and imperturbable to the end, and were for that very reason the most powerful men in the room.

They drank heavily, I should note, but it was as if the alcohol simply disappeared, evaporated, was not consumed. I could not say they were any drunker when we left than they were when we arrived. Cochocho, on the other hand, changed dramatically: became more desperate, less self-possessed, revealing in spite of himself the essential joylessness at the core of his being. His neatly combed hair somehow became wildly messy, his face swollen and adolescent, so that you could intuit, but not see, a grown man's features hidden beneath. No one liked him; more to the point, he did not like himself. And then there was Santos, who was of that generation that catches cold if they leave the house without a well-knotted necktie, who, like all retired, small-town teachers, had the gloomy nostalgia of a deposed tyrant. I caught him looking at Celia a few times with hunger—the hunger of an old man remembering better days—and it moved me. We locked eyes, Santos and I, just after one of these glances; he bowed his head, embarrassed, and looked down at his shoes, surprised and disappointed to find them without polish. He began to hate me, I could feel it. He expressed most clearly what the others were unwilling to acknowledge: that the visitors had upset their pride.

We'd reminded them of their provincialism.

Which is why I liked Santos the best. Even though the role I was inhabiting placed us at opposite ends of this divide;

in truth, I identified very closely with this wounded vanity. I felt it, would feel it, would come to own this troubling sense of dislocation myself. I knew it intimately: it was how the real Nelson felt in the presence of the real Francisco.

Hurt. Small.

Now the lights in the bar hummed, and the empty beer bottles were magically replaced with new ones, and my father's old history teacher aged before my eyes, souring, the color draining from him until he looked like the people in Raúl's old photographs. Jaime and Erick maintained the equanimity of statues. Cochocho, with his ill humor and red, distended skin, looked like the mold spreading on Raúl's kitchen wall. He'd removed his suit jacket, revealing dark rings of sweat at the armpits of his dress shirt. Santos was embarrassed for him; it was unbecoming for a man of his position. No one else seemed to notice. At a certain point, Cochocho asked about my great-uncle's house, and when my father said that he'd transferred the property to a cousin of ours, the deputy mayor responded with a look of genuine disappointment.

"You could have left it to your son," he said.

It wasn't what he really meant, of course: Cochocho probably had designs on it himself, some unscrupulous plan that would net him a tidy profit. But I played along, as if this possibility had just occurred to me.

"That's true," I said, facing my old man. "Why didn't you?"

My father chose this moment to be honest: "I didn't want to burden you with it."

And then the night really began to turn: my old man frowned as soon as the words had escaped. It was more of a grimace, really, as if he were in real pain, and I thought of those faces professional athletes make after an error, when they know the cameras are on them: they mime some injury, some phantom hurt to explain their mistake. It's a shorthand way of acknowledging, and simultaneously deflecting, responsibility. We sat through a few unpleasant moments of this, until my father forced a laugh, which sounded very lonely because no one joined him in it.

"A burden, you say?"

This was Santos, who, excluding a year and a half studying in France, had lived in the town for all of his seventy-seven years.

Just then Celia came to the table with two fresh bottles. "Sit with us," I said. I blurted this out on impulse, for my sake and my father's, just to change the subject. She smiled coquettishly, tilting her head to one side, pretending she hadn't heard correctly. Her old T-shirt was stretched and loose, offering the simple line of her thin neck, and the delicate ridge of her collarbone, for our consideration.

"I would love to," Celia said, "but it appears there is no room here for a lady."

She was right: we were six drunken men pressed together in a crowded, unpleasant rectangle. If more than two of us leaned forward, our elbows touched. If we'd been sitting in a canoe, we would have capsized. It was a perfect answer, filling us all with longing, and though we hurried to make room, Celia had already turned on her heels and was headed back to the bar. She expected us to stay for many hours longer, was confident she'd have other opportunities to tease us. Her mother glared at her.

But the men hadn't forgotten my father's insult.

"Explain," said Santos.

My old man shook his head. He wore an expression I recognized: the same distant gaze I'd seen that first night, when we'd sat up, drinking tea and looking through Raúl's old photographs. *Who are these people? What do they have to do with me?* My father wasn't refusing; he simply found the task impossible.

I decided to step in, playing the one card he and I both had: *I understand because I'm an emigrant too.*

"I think I know what my old man is trying to get at," I said. "I believe I do. And I understand it because I feel the same way toward the capital. He meant no offense, but you have to understand what happens, over time, when one leaves."

Santos, Cochocho, and the others gave me skeptical looks. Nor, it should be said, did my father seem all that convinced. I went on anyway.

"Let's take the city, for example. I love that place—I realize this is a controversial statement in this crowd, but I do. Listen. I love its gray skies, its rude people, its disorder, its noise. I love the stories I've lived there, the landmarks, the ocean, which is the same as the ocean here, by the way. But now, in spite of that love, when I have a son, I would not *leave* it to him. I would not say: 'Here, boy, take this. It's your inheritance. It's yours.' I would not want him to feel obligated to love it the way I do. Nor would that be possible. Do you understand? Does that make sense? He'll be an American. I have no choice in the matter. That's a question of geography. And like Americans, he should wake into adulthood and feel free."

I sat back, proud of my little speech.

"Ah!" Santos said, in protest. It was a guttural sound, a physical complaint, as if I'd injured him. He scowled. "Rank nationalism," he said. "Coarse jingoism of the lowest order. Are you saying we're not free?"

We fell silent.

For a while longer the bottles continued to empty, almost of their own accord, and I felt I was perceiving everything through watery, unfocused eyes. The television had been trying to tell me something all night, but its message was indecipherable. I was fully Francisco now. That's not true—I was an amalgam of the two of us, but I felt as close to my brother then as I had in many years. Most of it was internal, and could not have been expressed with any script, with any set of lines. But this audience—I thought back to the two antagonists and Joselito's mototaxi, the way they became fully invested in the scene the moment they realized they were being watched. I'd taken my brother's story and amplified it. Made it mine, and now theirs, for better or for worse. It was no longer a private argument, but a drama everyone had a stake in. I could have invented it line by line, filled it with convincing generalizations about America and her citizens, about Oakland and the great state of California, about the prospects of two immigrant businessmen, friends, trying to make money in a poor community divided by racial and ethnic tension. I felt good. Content. Seized by that powerful sense of calm one has when you have understood a character, or rather, when you feel that character has understood you. I felt very confident, very brash, like I'd imagined my brother to feel all these many years on his journey across North America.

I stood then, and confirmed what I'd begun to sense while seated: that I was very drunk. It was comforting in a way, to discover that all that drinking had not been done in vain. It was time to go. Celia and her mother came out from behind the bar, to clear off the table, and the other men stood as well. And this was the moment I as Francisco, or perhaps Francisco as me, pulled Celia close, and kissed her on the mouth. Perhaps this was what the television had been trying to tell me. She kissed me back. I heard the men call out in surprise, heard Celia's mother as well, shrill and protective, but entirely reasonable. After all, who was this young man? And just what did he think he was doing?

I placed one hand at the small of Celia's back, pulling her into me. The crowd continued to voice its disapproval, scandalized, but also—I felt certain—glad for us. The dance is complete. The virile foreigner has made his mark. The pretty girl has claimed her property. And it was the role of the gathered men to be appalled, or to pretend to be; the role of the mother to wail about her daughter's chastity when she herself had never been chaste. But when it was over, when she and I separated, everyone was grinning. The old men, my father, even Elena.

Celia and Nelson, most of all.

VERY LATE THAT NIGHT I called Rocío from the town's only working pay phone. No, I did not feel any guilt. I just wanted to talk to her, perhaps laugh and discuss her lover's murder. It must have been three or four in the morning, and I could not sleep. I'd begun to have doubts about what had happened, what it meant. A few hours before, it had all seemed triumphant; now it felt abusive. The plaza was empty, of course, just like the previous night, only more so—a kind of emptiness that feels eternal, permanent. I knew I would never come back to this place, and that realization made me a little sad. From where I stood, I could see the sloping streets, the ocean, the unblinking night; and nearer, the listing palm tree scarred with names. I would have written Celia's name on it—a useless, purely romantic gesture, to be sure—but the truth is I never knew her name. I've chosen to call her Celia because it feels disrespectful to address her as *the barwoman's daughter.* So impersonal, so anonymous. A barwoman's daughter tastes of bubble gum and cigarettes, whereas Celia's warm tongue had the flavor of roses.

Santos and Cochocho and Jaime and Erick left us soon after the kiss, and it was just me and my father, still feeling amused by what had happened, what we'd been a part of. We felt a little shame too, but we didn't talk about it because we didn't know how. Grown men with hurt feelings are awkward creatures; grown men who feel dimly they have done something wrong are positively opaque. It would've been much simpler if we'd all just come to blows. Santos and Cochocho wandered off, a bit dazed, as if trying to piece together a crime, as if they'd been swindled. My father and I did a quick circle around the plaza, and begged off for the evening. We never ate. Our hunger had vanished. I tried and failed to sleep, spent hours listening to my father's snores echoing through the house. Now I punched in the numbers from the phone card, and let it ring for a very long time. I wasn't drunk anymore. I liked the sound because it had no point of origin: I could imagine it ringing in the city, in that apartment I shared with Rocío (where she was asleep and could not hear, or perhaps she was out with friends on this weekend night), but this was pure fantasy. I was not hearing that ring at all, of course. The ringing I heard came from inside the line, from somewhere within the wires, within the phone, an echo of something mysterious emerging from an unfixed and floating territory.

I waited for a while, listening, comforted; but in the end, there was no answer.

WE LEFT THE NEXT MORNING; locked the house, dropped the key in the neighbor's mail slot, and fled quickly, almost furtively, hoping to escape without having to say goodbye to anyone. I had a pounding headache, and I'd barely slept at all. We made it to the filling station at the top of the hill without attracting notice, and then paused. My father was at the wheel, and I could see this debate flaring up within him— whether to stop and fill the tank, or head north, away from this place and what it represented. Even the engine had doubt;

it would not settle on an idling speed. We stopped. We had to. There might not be another station for many hours.

It was Cochocho's son tending the pumps. He was a miniature version of his father: the same frown, the same fussy irritation with the world. Everyone believes they deserve better, I suppose; and in this respect, he was no different from me. Though he was a few years younger than me, already the bitter outlines of his future were becoming clear to him. I didn't want to admit that just then, and I disliked him intensely. He had fat, adolescent hands, and wore clothes that could have been handed down from Celia's mother.

"So you're off, then?" the boy said to my father through the open window.

The words were spoken without a hint of friendliness. His shoulders tensed, his jaw set in an expression of cold distrust. There was so much disdain seeping toward us, so determined and intentional, I almost found it funny. I felt like laughing, though I knew this would only make matters worse. Part of me—a large part—didn't care: my chest was full of that big-city arrogance, false, pretentious, and utterly satisfying. The boy narrowed his eyes at us, but I was thinking to myself:

Goodbye, sucker!

"Long drive," said Cochocho's son.

And I heard my father say, "A full day, more or less."

Then Cochocho's son, to me: "Back to California?"

I paused. Remembered. Felt annoyed. Nodded. A moment prior I'd decided to forget the boy, had dismissed him, disappeared him. My mind had gone blank, and I'd turned away from Cochocho's unhappy son, casting my eyes down the hill instead, at the town and its homes obscured by a layer of fog.

"That's right," I said, though California felt quite far away—as a theory, as a concept, to say nothing of an actual place where real human beings might live.

"I used to work here, you know," my old man offered.

The boy nodded with sublime disinterest.

"I've heard that," he said. "But it belongs to us now."

My father didn't answer.

The tank was filled, and an hour later we were emptying our pockets for the bored, greedy soldiers. They were the age of Cochocho's son, and just as friendly. Three hours after that, we were passing through Joselito's hometown, in time to see a funeral procession; his, we supposed. It moved slowly alongside the highway, a somber cloud of gray and black, anchored by the doleful sounds of an out-of-tune brass band. The two men who'd fought over the mototaxi now stood side by side, holding an end of the casket, quite obviously heartbroken. Whether or not they were acting now, I wouldn't dare to speculate. But I did ease the car almost to a stop; and I did roll down my window and ask my old man to roll down his. And we listened to the band's song, with its impossibly slow melody, like time stretched thin. We stayed there a minute, not more, as they marched away from us, toward the cemetery. It felt like a whole day. Then we were at the edge of the city; and then we were home, as if nothing had happened at all.

EXTINCT ANATOMIES

I'D BEEN IN LIMA for the first half of the year. For two months—winter months in the Southern Hemisphere—I visited my cousin's dental office every Tuesday. I'd gotten financing for a recording project in Lima, and since I had no insurance back in the States, it seemed like a good time to get my teeth fixed. Before I left, my girlfriend let me know she approved.

"Maybe," she said, "it will make you more willing to smile."

My cousin and I had a standing appointment, which I kept at all costs. My case was a difficult one, he told me again and again, repeating it so often I began to take some pride in this. "How'd you break your front teeth?" he asked on my first visit, and without hesitating, I described a schoolyard fight I'd once observed—two brave, wiry boys pummeling each other with abandon. In my telling, I was one of the boys.

Interesting, my cousin said. He ordered X-rays, as if to confirm my story.

When I was a boy, my cousin lived with my family in Birmingham, Alabama. He went to the local public school, and most weeknights, one young lady or another would phone our house and ask to speak to—and here she would stretch out his name in an impossible southern drawl—and my mother, always severe, would correct her, then call it out loud. Upon hearing his name, my cousin would race to the kitchen like a man on fire, stretching the long cord into the hallway, where he'd spend an hour whispering his broken, seductive English into the receiver. In matters of flirting, he was a minimalist: "Oh, your hair," he'd say, or, "Oh, your eyes." I'd eavesdrop, unable to fathom what a girl might say in response to these cues. When it was over, he'd lock himself in the bathroom, emerge a while later showered and combed, and as we prepared for bed, my cousin, flummoxed and anxious, would ask me in Spanish: "What do American girls want?"

I was eight years old.

Now my weekly dental appointments were the only time we saw each other. We didn't talk much. I spent most of our time together with my mouth open, blinded by the overhead lamp, trying to block out the sound and sensation of the drill. I curled my toes in my shoes, or jammed my hands into my pockets and squeezed my wallet like a man being mugged.

I'm sensitive to pain, I told him on that first day, hoping he would be gentle.

He smiled. "I know," he said. "I remember from when we were kids."

My cousin's regular assistant was young, a novice, charged mainly with suctioning spit from my mouth with a transparent plastic tube. To accomplish this task she hovered close, blinking her gentle, unjudging eyes at me, and though I rarely saw her without a face mask, I'd begun, over the course of my long and complicated treatment, to imagine she was quite beautiful. My cousin sawed my teeth, chipped them, filed them, burnished them, polished them, bleached them, carved them, and all through this torturous process his assistant wiped spittle from my cheeks with an affectionate gesture and an invisible smile I'd come to crave. In the course of these endless appointments, I'd established certain routines, ones that involved sublimating the discomfort of the drill with thoughts of sex. I undressed my cousin's dental assistant with my eyes. My girlfriend had stayed back in the States, and though things were not well between us, I was attempting fidelity, and managing this famine only by giving myself certain creative license. How else to survive? There was nothing to look at but the assistant or the unadorned walls, and naturally I preferred to imagine what juicy lips were hidden behind her protective face mask. I tore off her white uniform—why not, I could see through it anyway!—bent her over the counter, and tongued her ear until it sparkled.

My cousin was planning to marry a woman named Carmen, who was finishing her last year of law school. She was lovely, short and curvaceous, and wore her dark bangs pressed diagonally against her forehead with a rigid Plasticine gel. Unlike American girls, she was quite clear about what she wanted. For starters: a church wedding. A white dress. A slow waltz before the entire family, and camera flashes popping from every direction. A bottle of whiskey on each table, and a tawdry night at the Sheraton in Miraflores, overlooking the sea. Later: a passel of children who'd study at the American school, a house with a room for the maid, and a garden to receive guests. These were things anyone could tell just by looking at her, perfectly reasonable goals in this city, and there were others too, which my cousin hinted at on occasion with a sly smile. *Oh, your hair,* I thought, *Oh, your eyes.* I kept my mouth open and listened as he told me of weekend visits to chapels all over Lima, how much they cost, how far in advance these houses of worship had to be reserved. Nothing aroused her more than wedding talk, he said to me, a fact he considered curious. He was enjoying himself so much he was hoping to postpone the wedding for another year, longer if possible.

It was early August, a busy day for both of us, and my cousin and I met in late afternoon. I had temporary caps on five of my teeth, two of which would be coming off that day. His dental assistant had gone home, he said when I arrived, and I contemplated with horror the sexless hour of dental torture that awaited me.

My cousin must have seen my anxious look.

"Don't worry," he said. "Carmen is coming."

"Oh," I said. "Isn't she a lawyer?"

He shrugged. Yes, it was true. Technically speaking, she was not trained. But was it that difficult? He spread his arms wide, as if embracing the entire room. "Is any of this really that difficult?"

"I don't know," I said.

He leaned in: "I studied in Oregon for three years, cousin. Three years. And you want to know the truth? I could have done it in two."

"Wow," I said, as he held up two fingers. A peace sign, half a set of air quotes, a pair of scissors.

Carmen arrived a few minutes later in a black miniskirt and a sky-blue wool sweater. She looked great, and this was precisely what I'd been afraid of. My cousin's dental office faced a major avenue, and at rush hour, traffic moved slowly and noisily, an unyielding army of gaseous vehicles. Rank fumes, blaring sirens, the intermittent screech of brakes. Even at eight in the evening, the bedlam had not eased. *I will think of the traffic,* I told myself, and it seemed like a solution: What could be more stifling to the human sexual impulse than these sounds, these smells, these tortured, broken-down, and dying cars and buses, these accidents-in-waiting, these flat tires and stolen mirrors, these dented doors and missing hubcaps, these potholed streets that cannot bear them all? I feel happy. Blissfully asexual. Then my cousin and Carmen put on their surgical gloves. She does not wear a face mask. The drill starts up. *I will not think of my cousin's wife-to-be,* I tell myself. *I will not think of her red lips, or notice how attentive she is, how tender when she leans over me to wipe my face, how her breasts just graze my arm.*

But something changes. A cap is removed with what amounts to a hammer blow, and the pain forces my eyes shut. I open them, and Carmen is staring: I offer her an ugly stump-toothed smile. She turns away, and now they are talking about the wedding as if I'm not there: the chapel, the floral arrangement, the priest, the readings. And I'm confused: my brain can't decide between traffic or sex, weddings or sex, white walls or sex, though none of these is actually within reach. Spit is running down my cheek, to my neck, where it soaks the collar of my sweater. It's warm. I'd like to think of my girlfriend, but I can't make her image appear. I'd like to think of my cousin's assistant, but she is halfway home by now, wherever home might be, sedated by the narcotic stop and start of a packed city bus. I'd like to think of Carmen, who is beautiful and demanding and doesn't notice or care that rivulets of spit have soaked into the chair now and are creeping south along my spine. There's a dress, she tells my cousin (not me, I'm not even there), a lovely white dress she's been looking at, and as she describes it in greater and greater detail—its lacy, open-backed elegance—I turn to my cousin, who withdraws a metal hook from my mouth and winks. I nod, I get the message, and in my mind, I'm pulling the hem of this not-quite-virginal dress up Carmen's thighs and burying my face between her legs. As if to punish me, my cousin takes out the hammer and bangs on my teeth. Another cap comes off, and now my smile is even more grotesque. They offer me a mirror, but I decline. Unfortunately, I know exactly what I look like. I'm far from home. My eyes burn. My cousin is distracted by all this wedding talk. He spends more time looking at his fiancée than at me. They are playing footsie beneath the reclining dental chair. I can't see it, but I know.

Then the drill strikes a nerve and I sit up, startled and wide-eyed.

Carmen stops in mid-sentence. Her bangs glisten.

"You're all wet," she says.

"Are you all right?" my cousin asks. "Has something happened?"

REPÚBLICA AND GRAU

THE BLIND MAN LIVED in a single room above a bodega, on a street not so far from Maico's house. It was up a slight hill, as was everything in the neighborhood. There was nothing on the walls of the blind man's room, nor was there anywhere to sit, and so Maico stood. He was ten years old. There was a single bed, a nightstand with a radio wrapped in duct tape, a washbasin. The blind man had graying hair and was much older than Maico's father. The boy looked at his feet, and kicked together a small mound of dust on the concrete floor while his father and the blind man spoke. The boy didn't listen, but then no one expected him to. He was not surprised when a tiny black spider emerged from the insignificant pile he had made. It skittered across the floor and disappeared beneath the bed. Maico raised his eyes. A cobweb glittered in an upper corner. It was the room's only decoration.

His father reached out and shook the blind man's hand.

"So it's agreed," Maico's father said, and the blind man nodded, and this was all.

A WEEK LATER, Maico and the blind man were in the city, at the noisy intersection of República and Grau. They had risen early on a winter morning of low, leaden skies, and made their way to the center, to this place of snarling, bleating traffic, in the shadow of a great hotel. The blind man carried a red-tipped cane, and he knew the route well, but once they arrived he folded the cane and left it in the grassy median. His steps became tentative, and Maico understood that the pretending had begun. The blind man's smile disappeared, and his jaw went slack.

Everything there was to know Maico learned in that first hour. The lights were timed: there were three minutes of work, followed by three minutes of waiting. When the traffic stopped, the blind man put one hand on the boy's shoulder and with the other held out his tin, and together they walked up the row of idling cars. Maico led him toward the cars with windows rolled down, and the blind man muttered helplessly as he approached each one. Maico's only job was to steer him toward those who were likely to give, and make sure that he did not waste time on those who would not. Women driving alone were, according to the blind man, preemptively generous, hoping, in this way, to avoid being robbed. They kept small coins in their ashtrays for just such transactions. Taxi drivers could be counted on as well, because they were working people, and men with women always wanted to impress and might let slip a few coins to show their sensitive side. Men driving alone rarely gave, and not a moment should be squandered beside a car with tinted windows. "If they know you can't see them," the blind man said, "they don't feel shame."

"But they all know you can't see them," Maico said.

"And that's why you're here."

Maico's mother hadn't wanted him to work in the city, had said so the night before, but his father had bellowed and slammed a fist on the table. Of course, these gestures were hardly necessary; in truth, Maico didn't mind the work. He even liked the pace, especially those moments when there was nothing to do but watch the endless traffic, soak in its dull roar. "Grau is the road people take to connect to the northern districts," the blind man explained. He had the city mapped clearly in his mind. There was money to be made in the north: it was a region of people trying to better themselves. Not like the southern rich, who had forgotten where they'd come from. "It's a generous intersection, this one," the blind man said. "These people recognize me and love me because they have known me their entire lives. They give."

Maico listened as well as he could above the din. *Me me me*—that was what he heard. The cars and the engines and the blind man; it was all one sound. Acrid fumes hung over the intersection, so toxic that after only an hour Maico could feel a bubble in his chest, and then, in his throat, something tickling.

He coughed and spat. He apologized, as his mother had taught him.

The blind man laughed. "You'll do much worse here, boy. You'll cough and piss and shit and it will all be the same."

The clouds thinned out by noon, but that morning was cool and damp. The blind man kept all the money, periodically announcing how much they'd collected. It wasn't much. Each time a coin was dropped into the tin, the blind man bowed humbly, and though he hadn't been asked to, Maico did the same. The blind man emptied the tin into his pocket when the light changed, and warned Maico to watch out for thieves, but the boy saw only men hawking newspapers and chalkboards, women with baskets of bread or flowers or fruit, and the very density of people in the area made it seem safe. Everyone had been kind to him so far. A woman his mother's age gave him a piece of bread with sweet potato because it was his first day. She tended to a few toddlers on the median. They were playing with a stuffed animal, taking turns tearing it to pieces. The stuffing spread across the grass in white clumps, and when a truck rolled by, these were blown into the street.

When the blind man found out that Maico had gone to school, he bought a newspaper and had the boy read it to him. He nodded or clucked his tongue while Maico read, and the stories were so absorbing that they even missed a few lights so that he could finish them. A judge had been murdered the previous day, in broad daylight, at a restaurant not far from where they sat. An editorial defended the life of a guard dog the authorities wanted put down for having killed a thief. There would be a new president soon, and protests were planned to welcome her. Music leaked from the windows of passing cars, and Maico could hear voices at each light singing along to a dozen different melodies. When he could, he studied the blind man's face. Unshaven and olive-skinned, with puffy cheeks. His nose was crooked and squat. He didn't wear dark glasses as some of the blind did, and Maico guessed that the sullen sheen of the man's useless gray eyes was part of his value as a beggar. It was a competitive area, after all, and there were others working that morning whose qualifications for the position were clearly beyond question.

MAICO'S FATHER WAS WAITING at the door of the blind man's room when they got back that afternoon. He winked at Maico and then greeted the blind man gruffly, surprising him. "The money," he said, with no warmth in his voice. "Let's see it."

The blind man pulled out his key and patted the door for the lock. "Not here. Inside is better. You people with eyes are always so impatient."

Maico stood by while they divided the take. The counting went slowly. The blind man felt each coin carefully, then announced its worth out loud. When no one contradicted him, he continued, his hands moving with elegant assurance, organizing the money into piles on the bed. A few times, he misidentified a coin, but Maico felt certain that this was by design. The third time it happened, Maico's father sighed. "I'll count," he said, but the blind man would have none of it.

"That wouldn't be fair, now, would it?"

When the counting was done, Maico and his father walked home in silence. It had taken longer than they'd expected, and Maico's father was in a hurry. He carried their cut in his pocket. When his mother asked how it had gone, his father sneered and said that there was no money. Or none worth mentioning. He prepared for his night shift while the boy and his mother ate dinner.

The second day, it was the same, but on the third, when they walked down the hill after his day with the blind man, Maico's father took the boy to the market and bought sodas for them both. An old gentleman with thick, calloused hands served them. Maico drank his soda through a straw. His father asked him how the work was, whether he liked it. By now, Maico was old enough to know that he should not say too much. He'd learned this from his mother.

Did he like downtown?

He did.

And was he enjoying the work?

He was.

What was it like?

Here, Maico chose his words carefully, explaining what he had absorbed in those few days. About charity, about traffic, about the relative generosity of cars headed north versus those headed south.

Maico's father listened calmly. He finished his soda, ordered a beer, then thought better of it. He looked at his watch, then scattered a few coins on the counter, and the old man swept them into his palm with a frown. "We're being robbed," Maico's father said. "Do you hear me, boy? You've got to keep track of the money. You've got to add it up in your head."

Maico was quiet.

"Are you listening to me? The blind man gets half. We get half."

The blind man had bought Maico a bag of popcorn that morning. After Maico had read him the paper, he had told stories about how the city had been when the air there was still sweet, when there was no traffic. The place he described seemed fantastical. "Even the intersection where we work was quiet once," the blind man had said, smiling, because he knew this would be hard to believe.

Now the boy looked up at his father.

"You can't let a blind man hustle you, son," his father said. "It's an embarrassment."

Maico did his best to keep an accurate count the next day, but by lunchtime the exhaust made him swoon. When he asked how much there was, the blind man said that he couldn't know for sure. "I'll count it later," he said.

"Count it now," Maico said. The words came out with a certain snap that the boy liked.

But the blind man just smiled. "Cute," he said. "Now read the next story."

A horn blew, and then another, and soon there was a chorus. When the street was quiet enough, Maico opened the paper again. An entire village in the mountains had been poisoned during a festival. Bad meat. The minister of health was airlifting in medicine and doctors. Then the light changed, and it was time to work.

Every afternoon, Maico's father was there to meet them at the door of the blind man's room. The money was never enough, and his father could not, or would not, hide his displeasure. Maico could sense it, knew with such certainty it was coming that when, on the eighth day, his father knocked the radio off the nightstand and said, "You stealing blind fuck!" he felt that he had willed it to happen. His father, angry, was a sight to behold: that great red face, eyes open to the whites, fists like mallets. Maico wondered if the blind man could truly appreciate the spectacle. Was his father's voice, the sharp edge of it, enough?

If nothing else, the blind man understood the seriousness of the moment. He seemed neither surprised nor afraid when his pockets were emptied.

The radio sputtered and died.

Until it stopped, Maico hadn't even noticed that it was on.

THEY WERE BACK AT WORK a few days later, with a new agreement. The boy would hold the money now. The coins weighed heavily in his pocket, so that the money felt like a lot more than it was. Just small, old, thin coins, worthless, worn-down coins, and when the work was done that day the blind man asked the boy to point him toward the hotel. It was sunny, and in the slanting afternoon light the hotel's glowing glass exterior seemed to be made of gold. "Now let's walk to it," the blind man said. He knew the way, and he had collected his cane, but here, in front of their regular clientele, it was understood that the boy should continue to lead him. They crossed Grau together, the blind man's hand on Maico's shoulder.

"On the far side of the hotel is a street. Read me the sign," the blind man said.

It was a narrow street. "Palomares," Maico said.

"Let's walk down this one, boy. Away from Grau."

When they had crossed the second intersection, the blind

man asked what was on each corner. Maico went clockwise: a bakery, a man selling roasted corn from a cart, an Internet café, a butcher shop.

The blind man smiled. "Behind the cart, what is there?"

"A bar."

"This bar—what's it called?"

"El Moíses."

"Let's go in."

It was quiet in the bar, and the blind man asked Maico to choose the best table. The boy picked one by a window. El Moíses was just below street level, and the windows allowed a view of people's legs as they passed. The smell of roasted corn on the cob filled the bar, and they hadn't been there long before the blind man gave in and asked for two. He'd already finished his first beer by then. He gave one ear of corn to Maico and washed the other down with a second cold glass of beer. He spoke wistfully of the fights that had exploded before him in this very same space: of chairs thrown, of bottles broken and brandished as weapons, of the beautiful noise of conflict. You could hear it in the breathing of those around you—panic, fear, adrenaline. There were a dozen names for that extraordinary sensation.

"What do you do when it happens?" Maico asked.

"Well, you fight, of course."

"But what do *you* do?"

"Ah, that's what you mean. How does a blind man fight?

I'll tell you." He spoke nearly in a whisper. "Recklessly. With whatever implement is at hand. Swinging wildly and searching desperately for an exit." The blind man sighed. "I suppose it's not so different for those who can see. More desperate, perhaps, or more reckless."

The waiter had turned on a radio, a low humming melody that Maico could not quite make out. They were the only people in the bar.

"Tell me," the blind man said, "what do you look like? I should have asked sooner. Describe yourself."

No one had ever asked Maico such a thing. In fact, it wouldn't have occurred to him that a question like that could even be asked. Describe himself. He thought for a moment, but nothing came to mind. "I'm a boy," he managed. "I'm ten years old."

"More than that," the blind man said. He took a swig from his beer. "I need more than that."

Maico squirmed in his chair.

"What does your face look like? I know you're small for your age. How are you dressed?"

"Normal" was all the boy could say. "I'm dressed normal. I look normal."

"Your clothes, for example, your shirt—what material is it?"

"I don't know."

"Can I touch it?" the blind man said. Without waiting for

an answer, he had already reached out and was testing the fabric of Maico's shirt between his thumb and forefinger. "Is the color very faded?"

"No," Maico said.

"Are there holes in the knees of your pants?"

"They're patched."

"And are the pants hemmed?"

"Yes."

The blind man grunted. "Your shirt is tucked in?"

Maico looked down. It was.

"And you're wearing a belt, I assume. It's leather?"

"Yes."

The blind man sighed. He called for another beer, and when the glass was placed on the table he asked the waiter to stay for a moment. "Sir, excuse me," he said, raising his right hand. He told Maico to stand, and then addressed the waiter again. "How would you describe the general appearance of this child?"

The waiter was a serious, unsmiling man. He looked Maico over from head to toe. "He's dressed neatly. He looks clean."

"His hair—is it combed?"

"Quite."

The blind man thanked him and told Maico to sit down. He drank his beer, and for a moment Maico thought that he wouldn't speak again. On the radio, a new song started up, a voice accompanied by a bright, ringing guitar, and the blind man smiled and tapped his fingers against the table. He sang along, hummed for a moment when he didn't know the words, and then fell silent altogether.

"Your old man thinks he's a tough guy," he said finally, after the song had finished and the waiter had brought him another beer. "Here's the problem. He goes off to work every night, and he doesn't see you in the morning, and, meanwhile, your mother dresses you. She must be a nice woman. Very correct. But you're a mama's boy. Pardon me, son, but I must speak plainly. That's why we don't make money. You can't beg looking like this."

Maico was silent.

The blind man laughed. "Are you taking this hard?"

"No," Maico said.

"Good. Very well." The blind man nodded, and whistled for the waiter, who appeared at the table and announced what was owed.

"Thank you, sir," the blind man said, smiling in every direction. "A receipt, please. The boy will be paying."

THAT NIGHT, Maico's father went into a rage. "Where's the money? Where's the money, you lazy little shit?" And what could he say except this: "I spent it," the sentence escaping on its own, and his fear arriving as soon as those three words and the half-truth they expressed were audible. Fear spread outward from his chest, so that his arms felt light and useless, his stomach watery, and then his legs would not hold him up any longer. His mother, when she tried to intervene, was beaten as well, and there was a moment in that short, furious episode— an instant—when Maico felt certain that he would not survive. His mother's screams told him that this was not like the other times, although if he had dared to open his eyes, he would have known it for himself from the savage look on his father's face. Then there was noise and there was light, and heat as if from a great exhaling fire. Maico peeked and the room itself seemed to move. He was pushed and he stood, and he was shoved and he surprised himself by standing again, and this continued until he no longer could.

All was quiet. Maico didn't know how much time had passed, only that his father had gone. He opened his eyes. The glass door of the cabinet had been shattered, a chair leg snapped. There had been a storm, and now it had passed; inexplicably, there was no blood. His mother leaned against the far wall, not sobbing, just breathing, and Maico crawled toward her, and then he slept.

Maico didn't dream that night. The few hours of sleep he managed were blank and dark. He woke at dawn in his bed. His mother must have moved him.

The blind man arrived the next morning, as if nothing had happened. Maico saw him and realized that he'd expected the man to be dead; he'd imagined that the fury his father had unleashed on him would be doubled or tripled for the blind man. Instead, the blind man wore the same contented look he'd had the afternoon before, when he left the boy at the bus stop, saying that he would make his own way home. There had been a softness to his words; he wasn't drunk, Maico knew, but happy, as happy as Maico was humiliated, as happy as Maico was angry.

"Go," his mother said. "Go. We need the money," and so Maico swallowed, and stretched his sore, wounded body. He stared angrily at the blind man, and then, with his mother sighing softly, he went.

Maico knew the way by then. Knew it well. Knew the names of the streets they passed on their descent to the center, the turns they took, the intersections where the road was rutted and the bus shook. All the sights along the way, the determined faces of the men and women who got off and on, and the collective breath the bus took as they crossed the bridge just before the old center. In the rainy season, the thin, dirty stream beneath them would come to life—or a kind of life— but for now it was just an anemic trickle that would not make it to the sea. Boys his age ran along the riverbed; Maico could see them from the bus, tending to their oily fires. If he'd been asked, he could have described it all for the blind man, this city of dirt and smoke, but Maico supposed that the blind man knew this place better than he ever would.

He didn't read the paper that day, didn't listen to the blind man's stories as the avenue filled and emptied according to its own somber rhythms. He waited for the blind man to apologize, though he knew that he wouldn't. He didn't bother to count the money before it disappeared into his pocket, and it was only when the skies began to clear, when the sun poured through a gaping hole in the clouds, that he realized that there had never been so much. Maico touched his face. His sore jaw, his bruised cheek, his right eye, not swollen shut but pinched so that he had to strain to keep it open. The blind man couldn't know. *Describe yourself. What do you look like?*

Beggar.

He was surrounded by them, could see them now, this itinerant army of supplicants, waiting for a stroke of good luck, for some generous act to redeem the day or the week or the month. Counting, hour after hour, the careful arithmetic of survival: this much for food, this much if I walk home, this much for the children, for the house, for the soup, for the drink, for the roof over my head, this much to keep the cold at bay. Maico's father spent his waking hours in another part of the city, engaged in much the same calculus, and if he had succeeded at anything, it was in shielding the boy from this.

"We're doing well today, no?" the blind man said. He didn't wait for an answer, just smiled and hummed a tune.

Then the light changed, and the boy gathered himself and led the blind man again through the idling rows of traffic.

The air was sweet with exhaust. A man driving alone dropped money into the tin. Maico stopped short. He turned to the blind man, faced him.

"What are you doing?" the blind man asked.

It wasn't a question that Maico could have answered, even if he'd tried. There was no question of trying. Maico reached into his pocket, pulled out the money they'd earned that morning, the money they'd been given, and dropped a handful into the blind man's tin, where it rattled wonderfully, heavily, falling with such abrupt weight that the blind man nearly let go. He said, "What's wrong with you, boy?" but Maico was not listening, could hear nothing but the sound of the revving motors, and he watched in the glare for the light to change; another handful of coins, little ten-cent pieces, the bigger silver coins that really meant something—all of it Maico dropped into the tin. He read the confusion on the blind man's face. The money was all gone now; he had none of it, and he began to step back and away from the blind man.

"Where are you going? Where are you?" the blind man said, not pleading but not unconcerned.

Maico steeled himself, and with a swift slap he upended the blind man's tin, knocking it and the coins from the beggar's hands and into the street. Some rolled under the idling cars, others nestled into the cracks in the pavement, and a few caught a glint of sun and shone and shone. But only for the boy.

A moment later, the light had changed, and the traffic had resumed its northward progress. But even if it had not, even if every car in the city had waited patiently for the blind man to drop to his knees and pick up each of the coins, Maico would have seen something that made it all worthwhile. It was what the boy would remember, what he would replay in his mind as he walked away, across the bridge, and up the long hill toward home. The blind man, suddenly helpless—for a moment, he was not pretending.

THE BRIDGE

TWO DAYS AGO, at approximately three forty-five Thursday morning, a truck driver named Gregorio Rabassa misjudged the clearance beneath the pedestrian overpass on the thirty-second block of Avenida Cahuide. His truck, packed with washing machines and destined for a warehouse not far from there, hit the bottom of the bridge, sheering the top off his trailer and bringing part of the overpass down onto the avenue below. The back of the trailer opened on impact, spilling the appliances into the street. Fortunately, at the time of the accident there were no other cars on that stretch of road, and Mr. Rabassa was not seriously injured. Emergency crews arrived within the hour, flooding Cahuide with light, and set about clearing the road of debris. Scraps of metal, pieces of concrete, the exploded insides of a few washing machines, all of it was loaded and carted away. Except for the ruined bridge, little evidence remained of the accident by the morning rush, and many people who lived nearby didn't even hear what happened while they slept.

The neighborhood to the east of Cahuide does not have one name, but many, depending on whom you ask. It is known most commonly as The Thousands, though many locals call it Venice, because of its tendency to flood. I've heard it referred to in news reports as Santa María, and indeed, it does border that populous district, but the name is not exactly correct. A few summers ago, after a wave of kidnappings, police dotted the area with checkpoints and roadblocks, and the neighborhood became known as Gaza, an odd, rather inexact reference to troubles on the other side of the world, only briefly and occasionally noted in the local press. How this nickname stuck is a mystery. The Thousands is an ordinary neighborhood of working poor, crammed with modest brick houses lining narrow streets. It is set in the foggy basin between two hills, and the only people who know it well are those who call it home. A turbid, slow-moving creek runs roughly parallel to Cahuide, and is partially canalized, a project intended to alleviate the annual flooding, but which has had, I am told, the opposite effect. The main road entering the neighborhood is paved, as are most others, but some are not. My uncle Ramón, who was blind, lived there with his wife, Matilde, who was also blind, and their road, for instance, was not paved.

On Thursday morning, my uncle and his wife left their

house early, as they always did; drank tea; and chatted briefly with Señora Carlotta, who sells emollients and pastries from a cart at the corner of José Olaya and Avenida Unidad. She tells me they were in good spirits, that they held hands as they left, though she can't recall what it was they spoke about. "Nothing really," she said to me this afternoon when I went to visit. Her broad face and graying hair give the impression of someone who has seen a great deal from her perch at the corner of these two rather quiet neighborhood streets. Her cheeks were wet and glistening as she spoke. "We never talked about anything in particular," she said, "but I always looked forward to their visit. They seemed to be very much in love."

Each working day, after drinking their tea and chatting with Carlotta, my blind uncle and his blind wife boarded the 73 bus to the city center, a long meandering route that took over an hour, but that left them within a few steps of their work. They were both employed as interpreters by a company whose offices are not far from the judicial building where I work: Ramón specialized in English to Spanish; Matilde, Italian to Spanish. All sorts of people are willing to pay for the service, and the work could be, from time to time, quite interesting. They would spend their days on the phone, transparent participants in bilingual conversations, translating back and forth between businessmen, government officials, or old couples in one country speaking to their grandchildren in another. Those cases are the most taxing, as the misunderstandings between two generations are far more complex than a simple matter of language.

I went to visit the offices yesterday on my lunch hour, to clean out their desks and talk to their colleagues. I have been named executor of their estate, and these sorts of tasks are my responsibility now. Everyone had heard about the accident, of course, and seemed stunned by the news. I received condolences in eight languages from an array of disheveled, poorly dressed men and women, who collectively gave the impression of hovering just slightly above what is commonly known as reality. Each interpreter wore an earpiece and a microphone, and seemed to have acquired, over the course of a career, or a lifetime, a greenish tint like that of the computer screen that sat before him. All around, the chatter was steady and oddly calming, like the sea, or an orchestra tuning up. One by one, the interpreters approached, shared a few hushed, accented words, all in a strange patois that seemed both related to and completely divorced from the local dialect. I had to strain to make out their words, and everything would end with an embrace, after which they would shuffle back to their desks, still lilting under their breath in a barely identifiable foreign language.

Eventually, an elderly gentleman surnamed Del Piero, who had worked in the Italian section with Matilde, pulled me aside, and led me to a bank of ashy windows that looked out over a crowded side street. He was bent, had a thin, airy voice, and his breath smelled strongly of coffee. His sweater was old and worn, and looked as if you could pull a loose strand of yarn and unravel the entire garment. Mercifully, he spoke a clear, only slightly accented Spanish. They had worked together for years. He thought of Matilde as his daughter, Del Piero told me, and he would miss her most of all. "More than any of these other people," he said, indicating the open floor of the translation offices with a disappointed nod. Did I hear him? He wanted to know if I could hear him.

"Yes," I said. "I hear you."

"She was a saint, a miracle of a woman."

I squeezed his arm, and thanked him for his kind words. "My uncle?" I asked.

"I knew him too." Del Piero shrugged me off, and straightened his sweater. "We never got along," he said. "I don't speak English."

I let this rather puzzling remark go by with barely a nod. We stared out the window for a moment, not speaking. A slow-moving line had formed along the wall on the street below, mostly elderly, each person clutching a piece of paper. Del Piero explained that on the last Friday of each month, one of the local newspapers held a raffle. Their offices were around the corner. You only had to turn in a completed crossword puzzle to enter. The man in a baseball cap leaning against the wall was, according to Del Piero, a dealer in completed crosswords. By his very stance, by the slouch of shoulders, you might have guessed he was involved in something much more illicit—the trade in stolen copper, the trafficking of narcotics, the buying and selling of orphans. I had barely noticed him, but now it was clear: the buyers came one at a time, furtively slipping the man in the cap a coin or two, and taking the paper he handed them. The old people rushed off with their answer key, to join the line and fill in the squares of their still-incomplete puzzles.

"What are they giving away this month?"

"How should I know?" Del Piero said. "Alarm clocks. Blenders. Washing machines like the ones that killed my Matilde." His face went pallid. "Your uncle wasn't blind. I know you won't believe me. But he murdered her, I just know he did."

Del Piero muttered a few words to himself in Italian, and then walked back to his desk. I followed him. "Explain yourself," I said, but he shook his head sadly, and slumped in his chair. He looked as if he might cry.

No one else seemed to notice our miniature drama, and I wondered if translators in this office often fell to weeping in the course of their labors. I grabbed a chair, and sat in front of his desk, staring at Del Piero as I do in court sometimes when I want a witness to know I will not relent. "Say it again. Explain it to me."

Del Piero raised a hand for a moment, then seemed to

reconsider, letting it drop slowly to the desk. There were beads of sweat gathering at his temples. The man was wilting before me. "What is there to explain? He could *see*. Your uncle moved around the office like a ballerina. I don't do anything all day, you know. No one speaks Italian anymore. Two calls a day. Three at most. All from young men who want visas, boys whose great-grandfathers were born in Tuscany, or Palermo, or wherever. And I negotiate with court clerks to get copies of ancient birth certificates. Do you realize that Italy barely existed as a nation then? All this fiction, all these elegant half-truths, just so yet another one of ours can flee! I know the score. They're all flying to Milan to get sex changes. Cheap balloon tits, like the girls in the magazines. Collagen implants. I can hear it in their voices. They're not cut out for life here. And so, what do I do? All day, I wait for the phone to ring, and while I wait, I watch them. The Chinese, the Arabs, the Hindus. I listen. I watch."

"What are you talking about?"

"He could *see*, damn it. I know this. Matilde and I would sit by that window, waiting for the phone to ring, drinking coffee, and I would describe for her what was happening on the street below. That swarthy guy in the ball cap—we talked about him every Friday! And she loved it. She said your uncle described things just as well. That he had a magical sense of direction, so perfect that if she hadn't known better, she would've doubted he was blind."

"He wasn't born like that, you know. He used to be able to see. What she said sounds like a compliment to me."

"If you say so." Del Piero looked unimpressed. "They're going to fire me now."

I didn't want to feel pity for him, but I couldn't help it.

He went on: "Matilde would have quit in protest. She loved me that much. And if she quit, your uncle would have too. He was their best worker—they never would've let him walk. His English was better than the Queen's!"

The Queen? I stood to go. "I appreciate your time," I said, though his phone had been silent since I'd arrived.

Del Piero caught me looking. "I got a call earlier. I might get another this afternoon." Then he shrugged; he didn't believe it himself. He walked me out, his sad, heavy eyes trained on the floor. At the staircase, he stopped. *"Coloro che amiamo non ci abbandonano mai, essi vivono nei nostri ricordi,"* he said.

"Is that so?"

Del Piero nodded gravely. "Indeed. It's not much, but it'll have to do."

I thanked him. Whatever it meant, it did sound nice.

RAMÓN LOST HIS SIGHT in a fireworks mishap at age seven, when I was only three. I have no memories of him before the accident, and to me, he has always been my blind uncle. He was my father's youngest brother, half brother actually, separated by more than twenty years, and you could say we grew up, if not together, then in parallel. By the time Ramón was born, my grandfather's politics had softened quite a bit, so the child was spared a Russian name. My grandfather lived with us, but I never heard him and my father exchange more than a few words. I spent my childhood ferrying messages between the two men—*Tell your father this, tell your grandfather that* . . . They'd had a falling-out when I was very young, a political disagreement that morphed into a personal one, the details of which no one ever bothered to explain.

Ramón's mother, my grandfather's last mistress, was a thin, delicate woman who never smiled, and when I was in elementary and middle school, she would bring her son over every week or so to see my grandfather. I was an only child in a funereal house, and I liked the company. Ramón made a point of addressing me as *nephew*, and my father as *brother*, with such rigor that I understood his mother had taught him to do so. I didn't mind. He always had a new dirty joke to share, something beautifully vulgar he had learned from his classmates at the Normal School for Boys in the old city center. He must've been fourteen or fifteen. A serious student of English even then, he would record the BBC evening news on the shortwave, and play it back, over and over, until he understood and could repeat every word. His dedication to the exercise always impressed me.

To my ear, the house got even quieter whenever Ramón and his mother arrived, but he liked our place for precisely the opposite reason: with its creaky wooden floors, he could hear himself coming and going, he said, and the space made sense to him. It was large, and the high ceilings gave the human voice a sonority that reminded him of church. Sometimes he would ask me to lead him on a tour of the place, just to test his own impressions of the house, and we would shuttle up and down the steps, or tiptoe along the walls of the living room so he could trace its dimensions. He had memories of the house from before the accident, but they were dimmer each day, and he was aware that his brain had changed. It was changing still, he'd tell me ominously, even now, even at this very moment. I thought he was crazy, but I liked to hear him talk. My mother had lined the stairwell with framed photographs, and Ramón would have me describe what seemed to be quite ordinary family scenes of birthday parties and vacations, my school pictures, or my father with a client celebrating some legal victory.

"Am I in any of them?" Ramón asked me once, and the question caught me so off guard that I said nothing. I remember a ball of pain in the hollow of my stomach, and panic spreading slowly up to my chest, my arms. I held my breath until Ramón began laughing.

He would have been forty-four this year.

The centerpiece of each visit was a closed-door sit-down

with my grandfather. They spoke about Ramón's studies, his plans, my ailing grandfather dispensing stern bits of wisdom gathered from his forty years as a municipal judge. I was always a bit jealous of these; the undivided attention my grandfather gave Ramón was something my father never gave me. But by the time I was ten, the old man was barely there, his moments of lucidity increasingly brief, until everything was a jumble of names and dates, and he could barely recognize any of us. In the twenty-odd years since my grandfather passed away, my father's mind has collapsed along a similar, if slightly more erratic pattern, as perhaps mine will too, eventually. My inheritance, such as it is. One day, after Ramón's conversation with my grandfather, he and I went on a walk through the neighborhood. I must have been twelve or thirteen. We were only a few blocks from my house when Ramón announced that he wouldn't be coming to visit anymore. "There's no point," he said. He was finishing school, and would soon be attending the university on a scholarship. We were walking in the sun, along the wide, tree-lined median that ran down the main avenue of my district. Ramón had a hand in his pocket, had insisted on going barefoot so he could feel the texture of the grass between his toes. He had tied the laces of his sneakers, and wore them slung around his neck.

"What about me?" I said.

He smiled at the question. "You're a lucky boy. You live with your dad."

I had nothing to say to that.

"Do you want to see something?" Ramón took his hand from his pocket, opening it to reveal a small spool of copper wire, bent and coiled into an impossible knot. I asked him what it was.

"It's a map," he said.

I took it when he passed it to me, careful not to disturb its shape.

"Every time we turn, I bend it," he explained. "And so I never get lost."

"Never?"

"I'm very careful with it."

"It's nice," I said, because that was all I could think to say.

Ramón nodded. "My father isn't coming back. Your grandfather. His mind has . . ." He cupped his hands together, then opened them with a small sound, as if he'd been holding a tiny bomb that had just gone off.

"The old guy's not going to miss me."

The sun was bright, and Ramón turned toward it, so that his face glowed. I couldn't deny that he looked very happy.

When we got back to the house, my grandfather was in the living room, asleep in front of the television, taking shallow breaths through his open mouth. He'd been watching opera, and now Ramón's mother sat by his side, combing his hair. She stood when she saw her son, nodding at me without a hint of warmth, and then gathered her things. She left the comb balanced on my grandfather's knee.

"It's time to go," she said. "Careful. Don't wake your father. Now say goodbye to your nephew."

He shook my hand very formally, and I saw very little of him after that.

My grandfather died two years later.

LAST NIGHT I couldn't sleep. For hours, I lay on my back, the bedside lamp on, admiring the ceiling and its eerie yellow tint. My wife slept with the blanket pulled over her head, so still it was possible to imagine I was all alone.

I thought of the truck, out of control and speeding, tearing the bridge down as it raced south. Or of Ramón, walking Matilde steadily, lovingly, to her death. In their haste, the local emergency crews neglected to block off the bridge's stairs on either side of the avenue. Four hours later, my uncle and aunt climbed these same stairs on their way to the bus stop, but they never made it, of course, tumbling onto the avenue instead, where they were killed by oncoming traffic.

It had been in all the afternoon papers on Thursday, along with photos of the truck driver, Rabassa, an unshaven young man with a sheepish smile, who wore his light brown hair in a ponytail. In interviews, he offered his heartfelt condolences to the families, but, on the advice of counsel, had little else to say about the accident. I would have given him the same advice. In the classic understated style common to our local journalists, the ruined bridge was now being called THE BRIDGE OF DEATH, or alternatively, THE BRIDGE TO DEATH.

At home, my wife and I instructed the maid to let the phone ring, and at the office, I asked my secretary to screen all the calls, and hang up on radio, television, or print reporters. It was only a matter of time, and by yesterday morning, when it was discovered that Ramón was related to my father, the scrutiny only intensified. There were now two scandals in play. In the afternoon, when I went to pick my daughters up from school, a young reporter, a boy of no more than twenty, followed me to my car, asking me for a comment, for anything, a phrase, a string of expletives, a word, a cry of pain. He had hungry eyes, and the sort of untrustworthy smile common to youth here: he could commit neither to smiling nor to frowning, the thin edges of his lips suspended somewhere in between. "Do you plan to sue?" he shouted, as my daughters and I hurried toward the car.

Last night I read the afternoon editions very carefully, with something approximating terror: What if someone had managed to get through to my father, to pry a comment from him? It would be difficult, given his situation, but not unthinkable, and surely he would oblige with something outrageous, something terrible. I bought a dozen papers, and read every page—testimonials from neighbors, interviews with civil engineers and trucking experts, comments from the outraged president of a community advocacy group and the reticent spokesman of the transport workers union, along with photos of the site—a hundred opinions through which to filter this ordinary tragedy, but fortunately, nothing from my father. There was nothing on the television either.

This morning, Saturday, I went to see my old man to tell him the news myself, and make certain the asylum's authorities were aware that soon the press would be calling. Apparently there had been attempts already, but I was relieved to discover my father had lost more of his privileges, including, just last week, the right to receive incoming calls. He'd long ago been barred from making them. Of course, there were some cell phones floating among the population of the asylum, so the secretary couldn't offer me any guarantees. She didn't know all the details, but his nurse, she assured me, would explain everything.

My old man has been in the asylum for three years now. He is only sixty-eight, young to be in the shape he's in. Every time I go, he's different, as if he's trying on various pathologies to see how they suit him. It happened so slowly I hardly noticed, until the day three and a half years ago that he attacked a man in court—his own client—stabbing him multiple times in the neck and chest with a letter opener, nearly killing him. It came as a great surprise to us, and the press loved the story. The scandal went on for months, and no aspect went unreported. For example, it was noted with evident delight that my father's client, the victim—on trial for money laundering—might serve time with his former lawyer if convicted. One columnist used the matter to discuss the possibility of prison reform, while a rather mean-spirited political cartoonist presented the pair as lovers, holding hands and playing house in a well-appointed prison cell. My mother stopped answering the phone and reading the papers; in fact, she rarely left home. But none of this chatter was relevant in the end: the money launderer recovered from his stabbing and was acquitted; my father was not.

His trial was mercifully brief. My old man, charged with assault and attempted murder, facing a prison sentence that would take him deep into his eighties, wisely opted for an insanity plea. Out of respect for his class and professional history, room was made for him at the asylum, and though it was jarring at first, over time he has become essentially indistinguishable from the other guests.

I was shown to the visitors' room by a pale, tired-looking nurse, who told me my old man had been in a bad mood recently. "He's been acting out."

I'd never seen her before. "Are you new?" I asked.

She walked briskly, and I struggled to keep up. She told me she'd been transferred from the women's pavilion. I tried to make small talk, about how things were over there, if she was adjusting to the inevitable differences between the genders, but she wasn't interested, and only wanted to tell me about my father. "He's a real sweetheart," she said, and she was worried about him. He wasn't eating, and some days he refused to take his medication. The previous week, he had tossed his plate at a man who happened to bump him in the lunch line. "It was spaghetti day. You can imagine the mess."

In case I couldn't, she went on to describe it, how my old man walked calmly from his victim, and sat down in front of a television in a corner of the cafeteria, watching a nature show with the sound off, waiting for the nurses to arrive; how when they did, he crossed his wrists and held his arms out in front of him, as if expecting handcuffs, which, she assured me, "we rarely use with men like your father." Meanwhile, a few terrified patients had begun to cry: they thought the victim was bleeding to death before their very eyes, that those were his organs spilling from his wounded body. The nurse sighed heavily. All sorts of ideas hold sway among the residents of the asylum. Some believed in thieves who stole men's kidneys, their livers, and their lungs, and it was impossible to convince them otherwise.

We had come to a locked door. I thanked her for telling me.

"You should visit him more often," she said.

A fluorescent light shone above us, cold, clinical. I kept my gaze fixed on her, until I could see the color gathering in her cheeks. I straightened the knot of my tie.

"Should I?" I said. "Is that what you think?"

The nurse looked down at her feet, suddenly fidgety and nervous. "I'm sorry." She pulled a key ring from her jacket pocket, and as she did, her silver cigarette case fell with a crash, a dozen long, thin smokes fanning out across the concrete floor like the confused outline of a corpse.

I watched her gather them. Her face was very red now.

"My name is Yvette," she said, "if you need anything."

I didn't answer.

Then we were through the door, and into a large, rather desolate common room. There were a few ragged couches and a pressboard bookcase along a white wall, its shelves picked almost clean, save for a thin volume on canoe repair, a yellowing Cold War spy novel, and some fashion magazines with half the pages missing. There were a dozen men, not more, and the room was quiet.

Where was everyone?

Yvette explained that many of the patients—she had used this word all along, not *inmates* or *prisoners*, as some others did—were still in the cafeteria, and some had retired to their rooms.

"Cells?" I asked.

Yvette pursed her lips. "If you prefer." She continued: and many were outside, in the gardens. The morning had dawned clear in this part of the city, and I imagined a careless game of volleyball, a couple of men standing flat-footed on either side of a sagging net, and quickly realized these were images drawn from movies, that in fact, I had no idea how those confined against their will to a hospital for the criminally insane might make use of a rare day of bright, limpid sun. They might lie in the grass and nap, or pick flowers, listen for birds or the not-so-distant sounds of city traffic. Or perhaps glide across the open yard, its yellow grass ceding territory each day to the bare, dark earth, these so-called gardens, each inmate just one man within a ballet much larger, much lonelier than himself.

My father preferred to stay indoors. Early on he wasn't permitted outside, and so had become, like a house cat, accustomed to watching from the windows, too proud to admit any interest in going out himself. In the three years I'd been visiting him, we'd walked the gardens only once: one gray morning beneath a solemn sky, on his birthday, his first after the divorce. He'd walked with his head down the entire time. I mentioned this, and Yvette nodded.

"Well, they're not exactly gardens, you know."

Just as Yvette was not exactly a nurse, this prison not exactly a hospital. Of course I knew. I watched a woman read to a group of inmates, what amounted to a children's story, and she could hardly get through a sentence without being interrupted. My father sat in his usual spot, by the high window in the far corner, overlooking a few little-used footpaths that wended between the trees surrounding the main building.

He was alone, which upset me, until I noticed that all the patients in this group were essentially alone, even the ones who were, nominally at least, together. A dozen solitary men scattered about, lost in thought or drugged into somnolence.

Yvette patted my arm, and excused herself wordlessly.

I made my way toward my father, past a small table along a salmon-colored wall that was stacked with games and pamphlets, and with a bulletin board just above it, announcing the week's program—POETRY NIGHT, SPORTS NIGHT, CEVICHE NIGHT. Hardly an evening passed, as far as I could tell, without a planned activity of some kind; it was no wonder these men seemed so tired. They all wore their own clothes, ranging from the shabby to the somewhat elegant, and this lack of uniform dress operated as a kind of shorthand, revealing at first glance which of these men had been abandoned, and which still maintained, however tenuously, some connection to the world outside. There were unkempt men in threadbare, faded T-shirts, and others who looked as if they might have a business meeting later, who still took the trouble to keep their leather shoes oiled and polished. A man in denim overalls sat at one of the two long tables writing a letter. An unplugged television sat at an angle to the small couch, its gray, bulbous eye reflecting the light pouring in through the windows. The curtains were pulled, but the windows themselves did not open, and the room was quite warm.

I sat on the windowsill.

"Hi, Papa," I said.

He didn't respond, only closed his eyes, gripping the arms of his chair to steady himself. He looked like my grandfather had so many years ago, shrunken, with long, narrow fingers, the bones of his hands visible beneath the skin. I hadn't seen him in six weeks or so. I asked him how he was, and he looked up and all around me, gazing above me and beyond me, with a theatrical expression of utter confusion, as if he were hearing a voice and couldn't figure where it was coming from.

"Me?" he asked. "Little old me?"

I waited.

"I'm fine," my father said. "A robust specimen of old age in the twilight of Western civilization. It's not me you should worry about. Someone snuck a newspaper in here two weeks ago. You can't imagine the scandal it caused. Is it true the oceans are rising?"

"I suppose so," I said.

He sighed. "When will the Americans learn? I can picture it—can you picture it? The seas on a slow boil, turning yellow, turning red. The fish rise to the surface. They feel pain, you know. Those people who say they don't are liars."

"Who says that?"

"Water heightens sensitivity, boy. When I was a child, I loved to sit in the bathtub. I liked watching my cock float in the bathwater and then shrivel and shrink as the water got cold."

"Papa."

"Sometimes it's so loud in here, I can't breathe. I will break that television if anyone attempts to turn it on. I will pick it up and break it over the head of anyone who goes near it. Just keep your eye on it. Just tell me if someone plugs it in. Will you do that, boy?"

I nodded, just to keep him calm, and tried to imagine the act. My father versus the television: his back would crumble, his fingers would crack, what remained of his body would collapse into a thimbleful of dust. The television would emerge unscathed; my father most certainly would not. When he spoke he waved his arms, fidgeted and shook, and even these small gestures seemed to be wearing him out. He was breathing heavily, his bird chest rising and falling.

"The nurse says you haven't been eating."

"The menu is not interesting," my old man said. He bit his bottom lip.

"And your meds? Are they interesting?"

He glared at me for a second. "Honestly, no. There is a gentleman here with whom I have made a small wager. He says there is a women's pavilion, not far from this building, full of loose women, crazier than hell. They tear your clothes off with their teeth. I say that's impossible. What do you know of it?"

"It's a beautiful day out, Papa. We could go out and see for ourselves."

"No need for that."

"What does the winner of this wager get?"

My father smiled. "Money, boy—what else?"

"I don't know anything about it, Papa," I said. "But I have some news."

At the sound of these words, after all the talk and movement, he fixed his stare on me, nodding, then closed his eyes to indicate he was listening.

"Ramón. Your brother Ramón. He's dead."

My father squinted at me. "The young one?"

I nodded. "Has anyone called you about this?"

He looked surprised. "Called me? Why would anyone call me?"

"The press, I mean. Have you talked to anyone?"

He dismissed the very idea with a wave of his hand. "Of course not," he said. "Am I in the papers?"

"The usual."

He smiled with a melancholy pride. "They don't get tired of me."

"I'm executor of the estate," I said.

"What estate? Ramón doesn't have an estate!" My old man laughed. "Let me guess . . . You're *honored*."

I could have hit him then. It happens every time I visit, and each time, I breathe, I wait for it to pass. And I think of my daughters, who will never see their grandfather again, and specifically of my youngest, who has no memories of him at all.

"How did it happen?" my old man asked.

And so I told him the story, what I knew of it—Rabassa's truck and the washing machines, the pedestrian bridge and the bus—as my father listened with closed eyes, letting his chin drop to his chest. As I recounted the events, the order of them, their inevitable conclusion, it sounded so asinine I felt he might not believe me at all. They had not been close. They had spoken little since my grandfather died, since my father had carved up the inheritance, keeping all that he could for himself. Ramón used his share to support his mother, and when she passed away, to buy the house where he and Matilde lived. There was little left over for anything else. My father's sister, my aunt Natalya, and his full brother, my uncle Yuri, pooled their shares together and bought a condo in Miami overlooking Biscayne Bay. My father got the bulk of the estate, of course, enough to live comfortably for many years, and that eventually covered his defense, the divorce settlement, his upkeep at the asylum. He even set aside a portion for me, his only child, which my wife and I used as a down payment on a house in a part of the city with only one name, and no pedestrian bridges. We have lived there since we were married eight years ago.

When I finished, he was quiet for a long moment, and seemed to be processing what I had told him. He could have just as easily been trying to recall who this brother was, and why it should bother him that Ramón was dead.

"She wasn't blind," my father said finally. "That bitch had cataracts, it's true, but she could see. She killed him."

For a moment, I couldn't say anything; I just stared at my father, wondering why I'd bothered. "Jesus," I said. "She sure seemed blind at the wedding."

My father looked at me. "How do you *seem* blind?"

"I was joking."

"Jokes," he said, disgusted. "I don't like your jokes." He stood abruptly. His shirt hung off him like a robe, and his belt had been pulled tight to the last hole, cinching his pants high above his waist, the fabric ballooning about his midsection. I reached to help him, but he shook me off.

"Papa, you have to eat," I said.

He ignored me, covered his eyes with one hand, and staggered toward the center of the room, a shaky arm raised before him. He stumbled toward the lesser of the two couches, where a nicely dressed gentleman sat thumbing through a pornographic comic book. As my father approached, the man cried out and fled. I called to my father, but he paid no attention, only changed direction, moving toward one of the tables now. There, the man writing the letter abandoned his work, and shuffled off to the corner of the room. The nurse who had been reading hurried over to see what was the matter, but I got to my father first, this blind, wobbling zombie; I put an arm around him, holding him gently, his thin frame, his hollow chest.

It took almost no effort to restrain him.

"I'm blind, I'm blind," he murmured.

I listened to the cadence of his breath. The other inmates had spread out to the pink corners of the room, as far as they could manage to be from my old man. They eyed one another tensely, and no one spoke. Just then, a black-haired nurse appeared before us. She wanted to know if everything was all right.

"Yes," I said, but my father shook his head. He cleared his throat, and it was only then that he dropped his hand from over his eyes, blinking as he adjusted to the light.

"Alma," he said, "my brother has died, and I am bereft. I must be released for the funeral. He has been murdered. It is a tragedy."

The nurse looked at my old man, then at me. I shook my head very slightly, hoping he wouldn't notice.

"Mr. Cano, I'm very sorry for your loss." Alma sounded as if she were reading from a script.

Still my father thanked her. "You're very kind, but I must leave at once. There are details to be taken care of."

"I'm afraid that's not possible."

"My brother . . ."

"Papa," I said.

"Mr. Cano, you cannot leave without a judge's approval."

I held my father, and felt the strength gather within him at the very sound of these words. He puffed up, his shoulders straightened. This was likely the least effective pretext one could give my father, the son of a judge, a man who had spent first his childhood and then his entire adult life wandering the corridors of judicial power, a man who had passed on to his own son, if little affection, at least much of this same access. He smiled triumphantly, and turned to me. "Your cell phone, please, boy. I know a few judges."

I pretended to search my pockets for my phone, as my old man watched me hopefully. By then Yvette had joined us, somehow gentler than I had noticed her to be at first, and she met his gaze, then touched his shoulder, and just like that he slipped from my hold, and into her orbit entirely.

"They've murdered my brother . . ." I heard my old man say, his voice mournful and low. Yvette nodded, leading him to the blue-green couch, and he went without a fight, collapsing onto it heavily. She kneeled next to him. Alma went off to soothe the other patients, who had been watching us with great anxiety, and just like that, I was alone. I could hear Yvette and my father murmuring conspiratorially, fraternally, now laughing tenderly, a voice breaking, now humming in unison what sounded like a nursery rhyme. With Alma's encouragement, the other inmates were spreading about the room again, in slow, tentative steps, as if trying to move without being seen. Yvette walked over to me.

"I'm sorry about your uncle," she said.

She glanced at my father, and then left us alone. I took her spot beside him, and together we watched the men drifting to their former places. The days here, I realized, are punctuated by these outbursts, these small crises that help break up the hours. These men had been socialized to expect discrete moments of tension, to defer to the impulse, whether theirs or someone else's, to fashion a disturbance from thin air. And they were experts too, at forgetting it all, at recovering, at turning back into themselves and whatever private despair kept them company. Except one of them: a slight, well-dressed man pacing back and forth in front of me and my father, occasionally pausing to flash us a confused glare. It took me a moment to realize what had happened: he carried a comic book in his right hand. We'd taken his seat.

I pointed him out to my father, and he shrugged. "I've never seen him before in my life."

"He was sitting right here."

"Of course. They were all sitting right here. And they can all sit right here again as soon as I get up."

"Papa, don't get upset."

"I'm not upset," he said, then corrected himself. "That's not true. I *am* upset. I would prefer he stop staring. It's rude. Tonight I will take his belt, and hang him with it."

I sighed. "Why would you do that, Papa?"

"I don't know," he said, his voice suddenly weak.

It was honest at least: he *didn't* know. My father remained, all these years later, the person most mystified by his predicament, by the actions and impulses that had brought him here. "It's okay, Papa." I tried to put an arm around him, but he shook me off.

"It's not okay. I'm going to die here. Not tomorrow, not next week, but eventually. The oceans are rising, and my blind brother has been murdered. My ungrateful son never visits, and my whore wife has forgotten me."

"Ex-wife," I said. I didn't mean to.

My father scowled, his gaze narrowing. "Whore ex-wife," he said. "Go. No one wants you here. Leave."

THE LAST TIME I saw Ramón was at a family party, about three years ago. It was my father's sixty-fifth birthday, his first since the arrest. This was before the divorce got under way, and my mother was still hanging in there. We decided to get my old man out for the party, just for the evening—not an easy task, but certainly not unheard of for a family of our connections, and our means. I was optimistic in the weeks before the party, and saw to it that my mother was as well. I thought it would be good for them both, to see each other, and especially good for him to be reminded of the life he'd once had. I paid courtesy visits to bureaucrats all over town, spoke elliptically about my father's situation and looked for the right opening, the right moment, to place money discreetly into the hands of those men who might be able to help us. But nothing happened: my calls went unreturned, the openings never came through. In the end, I had to tell my mother, only hours before the party, that the director of the asylum, whom I had spoken to directly and pressured through various surrogates, wouldn't take the bribe, just as no judge would sign the order, and no prison official would allow themselves to be bent. My father wouldn't be joining us.

She had spent a lifetime with him, and had become accustomed to getting her way. It was clear she didn't believe me. "How much did you offer?"

"More than enough," I told her. "No one wants to help him anymore."

My mother sat before her mirror, delicately applying makeup, her reddish-brown hair still pulled back. She had outlined her lips, and examined them now, getting so close to the glass I thought she might kiss herself. "It's not that. It's not that at all," she said. "You just didn't try hard enough."

That night Ramón arrived by himself, dressed as if for a funeral in a sober black suit and starched white shirt. His hair was cut so short that he looked like an enlisted man, or a police officer, and he had chosen to come without the dark glasses he sometimes wore. I'd never seen him this way. I was surprised to find him there, as was my mother, and for a moment much of the whispered conversation at the party had to do with his presence: Who had invited Ramón? How did he know? Why had he come? I led him through the thin crowd of friends and well-wishers, introducing him to everyone. *Oh, you're Vladimiro's younger brother,* some colleague of my father's might say, though for most of them, this was the first they'd ever heard of Ramón. If he noticed the chatter, he didn't let on. There were many fewer guests than we had imagined—even my uncle Yuri had called with an excuse— and the brightly decorated room seemed rather dismal with only a handful of people milling around. It was early yet, I told myself.

Ramón moved easily through the party, falling gracefully in and out of various conversations. He let go of my arm every time we stopped before a new group of people, holding his hand out and waiting for someone to shake it. Eventually, someone would. He held Natalya in a long embrace, whispering, "Dear sister, dear, dear sister." I left him chatting with my wife while I went for drinks, and our daughters, three and four years old at the time, climbed into his arms without hesitation. He beamed for a quick photo, and then released them, and measured their height against his waist. My wife told me later that he had remembered not only their names, but also their birthdays and their ages, though he hadn't seen them since my youngest was born.

My mother had positioned herself at the landing of the staircase, at one end of the large room, where she could survey the entire affair, and eventually we made our way over to her. Ramón asked me to leave them alone. They huddled together for a few moments, whispering, and when my mother raised her head again, her eyes were glassy with tears. She gathered herself, and called for everyone's attention. Ramón stood by her side. She began by thanking everyone for coming to celebrate this difficult birthday, how much it meant to all of us, to my father and his family. "We did what we could to have him here with us this evening, but it just wasn't possible," she said. She looked at me. "My husband has sent his youngest brother, Ramón, in his place, and I want to thank him for coming to be with us."

After acknowledging the polite applause, Ramón scanned the crowd, or seemed to, his lifeless gray eyes flitting left and right. There couldn't have been more than fifteen people altogether, everyone standing, waiting for something to happen. Someone coughed. Ramón asked that the music be turned down, cleared his throat, then went on to describe a version of my father I didn't recognize. A generous man, always available with a loving hand for his younger brother, a man who had helped guide and encourage him. Who had sat with him "after the accident that left me blind, the accident that made me who I am." My mother was sobbing softly now. "Vladimiro helped pay for my studies. He paid for my tutor, and helped me land the job where, by the grace of God, I was to meet my wife, Matilde." Then he raised a hand, and began singing "Happy Birthday," his voice clear and unwavering.

He sang the first line entirely alone before anyone thought to join in.

I found him, not long after, sitting in what had been my grandfather's favorite chair. He smiled when he heard my voice, he called me *nephew*. I asked him about life. It had been so long since we'd really talked. Matilde was well, he told me, and sent her regrets. They'd bought a house in the Thousands—*Where?* I thought to myself—and were talking about having a baby. He congratulated me on my family, and said, with a playful smile, that he could tell by the timbre of my wife's voice that she was still quite beautiful. I laughed at the compliment.

"Your instincts are, as ever, unfailing," I said.

We were—my wife and I—very happy in those days.

Ramón talked briefly about his work, which in spite of the feeble economy, remained steady: Italian was an increasingly irrelevant language, of course, but as long as America remained powerful, he and Matilde would never go hungry. Each day he took calls from the embassy, the DEA, or the Mormons. They trusted him. They asked for him by name.

We fell silent. The party hummed around us, and looking at our uncomfortable guests, I wondered why anyone would want to be part of our family.

"How did my father sound," I asked, "when you talked to him?"

Ramón ran his fingernails along the fabric of the armrest. "I didn't actually speak to him, you know. He had someone call me." He paused, and let out a small, sharp laugh. "I guess he couldn't get to a phone. I assume they're very strict about those things."

"I suppose."

"But then, I've heard you can get anything in prison," he said. "Is that true?"

"It's not exactly a prison, where he is."

"But he could've called me himself if he'd wanted to?"

I looked over my shoulder at the thinning party. "He's never called me, if that's what you want to know."

Ramón tapped his fingers to the slow rhythm of the music that was playing, an old bolero, something my father would've liked.

"That was quite a performance," I said. "Your speech, I mean."

"It was for your mother."

"Then I suppose I should thank you."

"If you like." He sighed. "My father loved Vladimiro very much. He was so proud of your dad, he talked about him all the time. He was heartbroken that they'd stopped speaking."

"Is that true?"

"Why do you ask if you won't believe my answer?" Ramón shook his head. "Do you visit him?"

"As much as I can."

"What's that mean?"

"As much as I can stand to."

Ramón nodded. "He's not an easy man. Matilde didn't want me to come. She has a sense about these things. And she's never wrong."

I thought he might explain this comment, but he didn't. It just lingered. "So why are you here?" I asked.

"Family is family." He smiled. "That's what I told her. She had quite a laugh with that one."

AND THEN, this afternoon, I went to Gaza. I took the bus, because I wanted to ride the 73, and sit, as Ramón and Matilde so often had, in the uncomfortable metal seats, beside the scratched and dirty windows, closing my eyes and listening to the breathing city as it passed. The air thickened as we rode south, so that it felt almost like rain, heavy, gray, and damp. The farther we went on Cahuide, the slower traffic became, and when I got off at the thirty-second block, beneath the remains of the bridge, I saw why. A stream of people filtered across the avenue in a nearly unbroken line: women carrying babies, stocky young men bent beneath the loads teetering on their backs, and children who appeared to be scampering across just for the sport of it. The median fence was no match for this human wave: already it had been knocked over, trampled, and appeared in places to be in danger of disappearing entirely. The harsh sounds of a dozen horns filled the street with an endless noise that most people seemed not to notice, but that shook my skull from the inside. I stopped for a moment to admire the bridge, its crumbling green exterior and shorn middle, its steel rods poking through the concrete and bending down toward the avenue. A couple of kids sat at the scarred edge, their legs dangling just over the lip. They laughed and floated paper airplanes into the sky, arcing them elegantly above the rushing crowd.

I walked up from the avenue along an unnamed street no wider than an alley, blocked off at one end with stacks of bricks and two rusting oil drums filled with sand. A rope hung limply between the drums, and I slipped under it, careful not to let it touch my suit. A boy on a bicycle rolled by, smacking his chewing gum loudly as he passed. He did a loop around me, staring, sizing me up, then pedaled off, unimpressed. I kept walking to where the road sloped up just slightly, widening into a small outdoor market, where a few people milled about the stalls stocked with plastics and off-brand clothes and flowers and grains, and then through it, to the corner of José Olaya and Avenida Unidad. There I found Carlotta.

The lawyer who'd called me yesterday with the news had advised me to look for a woman at a tea cart. She can show you the house, he said over the phone. Your house. That afternoon, as promised, a courier came by with Ramón's keys, along with a handwritten note from the lawyer once again reiterating this small piece of advice: *Look for Carlotta,* the note read, though there was no description of her. *You'll never find the house without help.*

In fact, it did all look the same, each street identical to the last, each house a version of the one next to it. Carlotta was sitting on a small wooden stool reading a newspaper when I walked up. I introduced myself, and explained that I needed to take a look at my uncle's house. She stood very slowly and wrapped me in a tight embrace. "They were so wonderful," she said. She kept her hand on mine, and didn't let go, just stood there, shaking her head and murmuring what sounded like a prayer. I waited for her to finish. Finally, she excused herself, went inside the unpainted brick house just behind her, and emerged a few moments later dragging a boy behind. He was eighteen or so, skinny, and looked as if he'd just been sleeping. He wore unlaced white high-top sneakers with no socks, and his thin, delicate ankles emerged from these clownish shoes with a comic poignancy. Her son, Carlotta explained, would watch the stand while we went to Ramón and Matilde's house. It wasn't far. The boy glanced in my direction through red, swollen eyes, then nodded, though he seemed displeased with the arrangement.

As Carlotta and I walked up the street, she pointed out a few neighborhood landmarks: the first pharmacy in the area; the first Internet kiosk; an adobe wall pockmarked with bullet holes, site of a murder that had made the news a few years ago. A police checkpoint, from the days when the name Gaza came into use, had stood right at the intersection we strolled through now. These were peaceful times, she said. She showed me the footbridge that crossed over the canal, and the open field just beyond it, where the turbid floodwaters gathered once a year or so. It was where the teenagers organized soccer tournaments, where the Christians held their monthly revivals, and where a few local deejays threw parties that lasted until first light. Awful music, she said, like a blast furnace, just noise. Her son had been at one of those, she told me, just last night. He was her youngest boy. "He's not a bad kid. I don't want you thinking he's trouble. Do you have children?"

"Two daughters."

She sighed. "But girls are different."

We turned left just before the footbridge, and walked a way along the canal, then turned left again to the middle of the block, stopping in front of a saffron yellow house. It was the only painted one on the entire street.

"It's yellow," I said to Carlotta, disbelieving. "Why is it yellow?"

She shrugged. "He did translations, favors. People paid him however they could."

"By painting a blind man's house?"

Carlotta didn't seem to find it that funny, or remarkable at all. "We called your uncle 'Doctor,'" she said, and gave me a stern look. "Out of respect."

I said nothing. There was a metal gate over the door and two deadbolts, and it took a moment to find the right keys. I'd never been to their house before, and I felt suddenly guilty visiting for the first time under these circumstances. Just inside the door there were a jacket and hat hanging from a nail, and below it, a small, two-tiered shoe rack containing rubber mud boots, beige men's and women's slippers, and two pairs of matching Velcro sneakers. There were a couple of empty spaces on the rack. For their work shoes, I supposed, the ones they had died in. Without saying a word, Carlotta and I left our shoes behind, and walked on into the house wearing only our socks. We didn't take the slippers.

The space was neatly laid out, as I had assumed it would be, and dark, with no lightbulbs anywhere and no photos, not of family, not of each other. Because the long, damp winters are even longer and damper in this part of the city, heavy translucent plastic sheeting hung from every doorway in wide strips, so that moving from one room to another required a motion not unlike swimming the butterfly stroke. The idea was to trap heat in each room, but the effect, along with the hazy light, was to give the house the look and feel of an aquarium. I parted the plastic curtains, and found myself in a sparsely furnished kitchen, kept in meticulous order. The refrigerator was nearly empty, and there were no extra utensils in the drawers, just a pair of everything—two forks, two spoons, two steak knives. I opened the tap and a thin line of water dribbled into a single dirty bowl. There was another one, a clean bowl already dry, sitting by the sink.

I walked to the bedroom, as spare and clean as the kitchen, where a small wooden cross hung just above the neatly made bed. I opened and closed a few drawers, looked into the closet, and found two pairs of glasses in a box on top of the dresser, one with plastic yellow lenses, one with blue. I tried on the yellow pair, charmed by this small evidence of my uncle's vanity, and even found myself looking for a mirror. Of course, there wasn't one. *This is all mine,* I thought, *to dispose of as I see fit. To sell, or rent, or burn, or give away.* There was nothing of my family in this house, and maybe that was the only attractive thing about it. My father kept everything of any value, and Ramón got everything else, all this nothing— these clothes, this cheap furniture, this undecorated room and nondescript house, this parcel of land in a neighborhood whose name no one could agree on. It was all paid for, the lawyer told me, they owned it outright, and my uncle had no debts to speak of. Unfortunately, he also had no heirs besides his wife, and she had none besides him. I was the nearest living relative.

After a long pause, the lawyer added: "Well, except for your father."

"What do I do with it?"

"See if there's anything you want to keep. You can sell the rest. It's up to you."

And now I was here, hidden in the Thousands. At home, my phone was ringing, the city's frantic journalists demanding a statement. Soon they would be camping out in front of the asylum, tossing handwritten notes over the walls and into the gardens, or crowding before the door to my house, harassing my children, my wife. Say something; entertain us with your worries, your fears, your discontent, blame your father, the men who built the bridge, or the ponytailed truck driver. Blame your blind uncle, his blind wife, the fireworks vendors, or yourself. My head hurt. *I miss Ramón,* I thought, and just as quickly the very idea seemed selfish. I hadn't seen him in years.

Carlotta had stayed in the living room, and from the hallway I watched her blurred outline through the plastic. I swam through the house to see her.

"Are you all right?" I asked. "I'm sorry to make you wait."

She had nested into the soft cushions of my uncle and aunt's white sofa. There was a throw rug on the floor, somewhere near the middle of the room, and the soles of her feet hung just above, not touching it. Her hands lay in her lap. She seemed much younger in the subdued light of my uncle's home, her skin glowing, and her hair, graying in the daylight, appeared, in this shadowed room, to be almost black.

"What are you looking for?" she asked.

It was a fair question, for which I had no answer.

"Nothing," I said. "Maybe I could live here."

Carlotta smiled generously. "You're not feeling well," she said.

My wife would be surprised this evening when I told her about my day. She listened patiently as we prepared a meal, our daughters clamoring for our attention, and told me only that I must be careful. That places like that weren't safe. She'd never been to The Thousands or Venice or Gaza, but like all of us, believed many things about our city without needing them confirmed. Hadn't there been a famous murder there a few years ago? And didn't this latest accident only prove again that our world had nothing to do with that one? And I agreed quietly, "Yes, dear, you're right, he was my uncle, my brother, but I barely knew him"—and I stopped my story there. I walked around the counter, gave her a kiss on the neck, picked up my eldest daughter, and laughed: Ramón's yellow glasses, can you believe it? His blue ones? His yellow house? And we put the girls to sleep, my wife went to bed, and me, I stayed in the living room, watching television, flipping channels, thinking.

"What will you do with it all?" my wife asked as she leaned against the doorjamb already in her nightclothes, and I could see the graceful outline of her body beneath the fabric. She was barefoot, her toes curling into the thick carpet.

"I was thinking we should move there," I said, just to hear her horrified laughter.

She disappeared into the bedroom without saying good night.

"Did you know them well?" I asked Carlotta.

She thought about this for a second. "They were my neighbors."

"But did you know them?"

"I saw them every day," she said.

And this means a good deal, I know it does. There was a time when I saw him every week, and we were closer then, maybe even something like brothers. "Ramón and I grew up together. And then we lost touch."

"You look tired," Carlotta said. "Why don't you sit? It might make you feel better."

But I didn't want to, not yet. I went to the record player, lifted the dull plastic dustcover. A few dozen old LPs leaned against the wall, and I thumbed through them: they were my grandfather's opera records. I put one on, a woman's elegant voice warbled through the room, and just like that, this melody I hadn't heard in so long—decades—dropped my temperature, and made the ceiling seem very far above me, at an unnatural height. Carlotta tapped her toe to the music, though it seemed utterly rhythmless to me. It was true: I didn't feel well.

"What did people think of them in the neighborhood?" I asked.

"Everyone loved them."

"But no one knew them?"

"We didn't have to know them."

And I thought about that, as the singing went on in Italian, a lustrous female voice, and I was struck by the image of the two of them—Ramón and Matilde—sitting on this very same couch, my aunt whispering translations directly into his ear. Love songs, songs about desperate passion, about lovers who died together. I could almost see it: his smile lighting up this drab room, Matilde's lips pressed against him. They had died that way, best friends, strolling hand in hand off the edge of a bridge, until they sank. I sat down on the throw rug, leaning back against the sofa, staring ahead at an unadorned wall. My feet were very cold. My eyes had adjusted to the light now, and the house seemed almost antiseptic. Clean. Preposterously dustless for this part of the city. We sat listening to the aria, Carlotta and I, a melody spiraling out into the infinite. The singer had such energy, and the more she drew upon it, the weaker I felt. I could stay here; I might never leave. *I could inherit this life my uncle had left behind, walk away,* I thought, *from my old man and his venom.*

"My father did everything he could to ruin my uncle," I said. "He cheated him out of his inheritance. He's in prison now, where he belongs."

"I know. I read about him today in the paper. They talked to him."

For a moment I thought I had misheard. "What? Which paper?"

I turned to see Carlotta smiling proudly. Perhaps she hadn't heard the terror in my voice. Already I'd begun imagining all the horrible things my father might say, the conspiracy theories, the racist remarks, the angry insults with which he might have desecrated the memory of his dead brother.

"I don't remember the name of it," Carlotta said. "The same one I was in."

"What did my father say?"

"There were journalists all over the neighborhood yesterday. My son was on television. Did you see him?"

I raised my voice, suddenly impatient: "But what did he say?"

"Mr. Cano," Carlotta whispered.

Her shoulders were hunched, and she had leaned back into the couch, as if to protect herself, as if I might attack her. I realized, with horror, that I had frightened her. She knew who my father was. I stammered an apology.

She took a deep breath now. "He said he didn't have a brother. That he didn't know anyone named Ramón."

"That's all?" I asked, and Carlotta nodded.

"No one named Ramón," I said to myself, "no brother."

She stared at me like I was crazy. How could I explain that it didn't sound like him, that it was too sober, too calm?

"Why would he say that?" Carlotta asked.

I shook my head. I felt my eyes getting heavier. Was it cruel or just right? "We should go," I said, "I'm very sorry, there's nothing here I need," but it wasn't true, and I couldn't leave. We sat, not speaking, not moving, only breathing, until I became aware that Carlotta was patting my head with a maternal affection, that my shoulders were sinking farther toward the floor, and I gave into it: loosened my tie, wiggling my toes in my socks, my feet frozen, the chill having spread through my body now.

This record will not end, I thought, I hoped, but then it did: a long, fierce note held without the orchestra, culminating in a shout of joy from the singer, the audience chastened, stunned by the beauty of it. A long silence, and then slowly, applause, soft at first, then waves of it, which on this old recording came across like a pounding rain. I was shivering. There was no question we were underwater.

THE LORD RIDES
A SWIFT CLOUD

THE TOWN ITSELF was interesting enough, with crumbling houses and narrow streets full of people who seemed not to know how to hurry. I learned to walk slowly and so this pace was not difficult for me. That day was absurdly sunny. In the afternoon I rode one of the funiculars to the top of a hill, an outcropping of rock high above the sea where the wind blew so hard it forced my eyes shut and dusted my face with a fine film. From there, between gusts, I could see the port, its gleaming metal claws, its workers scurrying between acres of containers stacked one on top of the other. Beyond it was the ocean, a beautiful, roiling sheet of silver.

Of course, the real work of the day was pretending I wasn't lonely. By late afternoon I had given up, so I went to a bar down in the flats, a place that looked and smelled like the inside of a ship: the air was sooty and humid, the walls were held up by wooden beams curved like ribs. At any moment I thought they would give and the ocean would leak through, slowly at first, then with a deafening crash, and drown us all. There were five or six men at the bar. None sat together.

Nearly every inch of the place was covered with photographs: of politicians and starlets, soccer players and singers. The wall behind the bar was reserved for portraits of garlanded racehorses and their jockeys. I read for a bit, but the light was dim and I could barely make out the words. There was no music and very little conversation. The men nodded at the bartender, and drinks appeared before them in almost soundless transactions. I was there an hour before anyone said a word to me. It was an older gentleman in a worn navy sport coat. He said: "You read so beautifully."

The way I felt in those days, it wouldn't have surprised me in the slightest to discover that I'd been reading aloud. I blanched. "How do you know?"

"You're so *still*."

Which struck me as funny. I'd been traveling at that point for eight weeks and already the town was fading. The next day I would be heading south, relentlessly southward, and in ten days I would be home again for the first time in two years. But I suppose everything about me gave the impression of a wounded man, determined not to move. I had not spoken to my wife in many months. The effort it took not to think of her was so great that in the evenings my bones ached.

"Cheers," I said.

He told me his name was Marcial. "I'm retired," he said. "It's wonderful." He paused, as if expecting me to respond, but I didn't. I must have glanced down at my book again. "May I?" he asked.

He was unshaven and had a tired look to him. His hair was completely, shockingly white. I passed him the book. It was all so tactile: he felt its texture, fanned its pages roughly, and smiled at the satisfying sound they made. He commented on the novel's weight. There was a woman on the cover, a stern, dark-haired beauty, looking down a Paris street. Or something like that. He ran his index finger over her face. "She's pretty," he said.

We clinked glasses. "I want you to understand my story," Marcial said. "When my wife died, I told our children that I would drink for a year and then find a new woman."

It was difficult to tell in the low light if he was a man at the beginning or the end of a yearlong bender. "How is that working out?"

His beard was growing in white. He scratched the stubble. "Very well," he said. "I have three months to go."

Eventually a television came on, and I pretended to read while Marcial followed a soccer match with muted enthusiasm. There was a red team and a blue team. When pressed, I sided with red, and this was met with approval. A few more people came in, some others left, but the real story I want to tell here is about how this man followed me home. It was late when I finally left, but it seemed much later. It seemed, in fact, like it should already be morning. It was a short walk to the hotel. As I gathered myself to go, Marcial pulled a few bills from his coat pocket and dropped them on the bar.

"No tip?" the bartender said. He was a dour man in his fifties, thin and balding, who had watched the entire soccer match without a sound, his hands folded neatly in his lap.

Marcial turned to me. "This man is the owner. I can't tip him because it would be an insult. Tips are for workers."

"What logic," the owner said. "There are other bars in town."

"But this one is special," Marcial said. He winked at me.

I paid and said my goodbyes. Marcial must have walked out right behind me, but a low, heavy fog had blown in, so I didn't notice him until I had reached the door of the hotel. He was ten paces back, shuffling up the hill. When he saw that I had seen him, he shrugged and, with great slowness, sat down on the curb, stretching his legs into the empty street. "I'm not following you," he said. "Just so you know. I've come to look at the park."

Across the street, bathed in fog, there was indeed a tiny, manicured park, with regal stone benches and neatly trimmed rosebushes. Somehow I hadn't noticed it that morning. It seemed to have been dropped in from another country, an imitation of a postcard sent from far, far away.

"There was a building there," Marcial said. "It wasn't a

nice building. It was a dump. Full of Czechs and Russians, and the whole world knows they're slovenly people. But in the alley behind it—can you picture this?—where the wooden fence is now." He pointed. "There! I kissed my wife in that spot when we were seventeen. We scratched our names in the bricks with my switchblade. Of course, you had to carry a knife in those days, not like now." He said this last line in a tone of great disappointment. "For example, you don't carry a knife, do you?"

"No," I said.

Marcial took a pack of cigarettes from his pocket and lit one without offering. His white hair seemed to glow. "I like your country," he said, though I hadn't told him where I was from. He blew smoke and stared into the street. "Fine contraband. Interesting climate. Lovely, generous women."

This entire time I'd been standing at the door of the hotel. I had the key in my hand and I could have left him at any moment.

"You're from the capital?" he asked.

"Born and raised."

Marcial sighed. "There's not a sadder, more detestable city in the world."

"You may be right," I said.

"Of course I am. Won't you sit?"

It was, in spite of the damp, a warm night.

"Why sugarcoat it?" Marcial said, once I had joined him on the curb. "I need money."

"I don't have money."

"Don't you?" He flicked what was left of his cigarette into the street. "The port works all night, you know, twenty-four hours a day. It never closes. Everything brought into this cursed country comes through there. Have you read the papers? These are the good times! So much work, and still they won't have me. Do you think I'm old?"

I shook my head.

My grandfather was the oldest person I've ever known. By the time I met Marcial he'd been dead for three years. I told Marcial how my grandfather had kept a girlie calendar in his workshop, hidden from my grandmother behind a more respectable one with pictures of our country's various tourist attractions: those ruins with which we tempt the world. When I was a boy, he had me pencil in my birthday on the hidden calendar. Even then his memory was fading. "It's in May," he said, "isn't it?" He held the calendar in his trembling hands and admired the woman. She was dark-skinned and leggy. My grandfather, I recall, held the calendar very close to his face; his eyes were no good. Then he passed it to me. "Go ahead, write it. And your name too."

"The problem is that my birthday is in March," I told Marcial.

He smiled. "But I forget things too."

A scruffy red-haired mutt appeared from under a park bench, padding lazily through the fog. He came right up to us, not growling, not afraid. Marcial took a wine cork from his pocket and held it out. The dog ventured closer, and licked the reddish end of the cork happily, like a lollipop. Marcial petted the dog with his other hand.

"You really must see the port at night. It's something else," Marcial said. "With all the lights, it looks like noon there. I can take you. I know the way."

"No, thank you," I said. Of course, every road in town led to the port, but it didn't seem right to tell him that.

He scowled. "You people have no appreciation. It's why you're so backward."

And with that, it was time to go. I was about to stand when Marcial stopped me. "Wait," he said, and I did. He shooed the dog away, as if he suddenly wanted privacy. He gave it a soft push, and when it resisted, he tossed the red wine cork down the street. The dog went off after it. He put his left hand on my shoulder, smiled, then showed me his right: it was a fist, and in it Marcial held a knife. It wasn't a long blade. He frowned. "You see, I was hoping to rob you this evening."

THAT NIGHT I DREAMED of her and woke in a panic. The next night I was in a different hotel, in a different town farther down the coast—the same dream. By the fourth night, I had come to distrust myself, and was barely sleeping. I was thirsty all the time. I finished the book I'd been reading and left it on the table at a coffee shop at a border town. I was halfway down the block when someone tapped me on the shoulder. It was the pretty waitress from the café. She was out of breath and there was a wonderful pink to her cheeks. "You forgot your book," she said.

"I left it on purpose."

She bit her lip. Somehow I'd made her nervous. "But you can't do that," she said.

And so I took it with me. Five days later, I was home. I still hadn't slept, and it took the last of my strength to open the windows of the shuttered apartment. These were the abandoned rooms where I had been raised. The entire family had filtered north, then my wife and I came back to live out the last days of our marriage. There was hardly any furniture left—little by little our neighbors had raided the place. When my father first complained, we attributed it to his dementia, but it turned out he was right. Now it had gotten out of control. The creaky chair where my wife and I had made love was gone. The sofa too had disappeared, and the wall clock, and the leather table in the foyer. I made a quick inventory: the china was missing, my mother's nice flatware, a silver picture frame, half the books. My grandfather's old tube radio was nowhere to be found, and there was a dish towel moldering where the television had once sat.

But what did I care? I emptied my bag on the floor of the

living room, shook its contents out, and observed with some satisfaction the accumulated mound of wrinkled clothes and paper and trinkets: train tickets, matchbooks, the knife I had taken from Marcial that night. The book was there too, adorned with its photograph of a Parisian woman with dark hair and dark eyes. It was summer and the setting sun poured in and stained the walls red. I could smell the ocean. Everyone knew I was back. I had sent postcards at every stop along the way, keeping the family apprised of my southern progress, and so I waited, watching the daylight fade, for someone to call. They were about to call; I was certain of it. There were, I assumed, still friends and family in this city of mine. I fell asleep on the wooden floor, waiting. When I awoke it was night, the apartment was dark and cool, and the phone hadn't disturbed my rest. I turned on every light in the old apartment and spent a furious half hour looking for it, tearing through what remained of our things, opening every drawer, every closet. The phone, the phone—our neighbors had taken it too.

THE AURORAS

✄ DARKNESS ON ALL SIDES ✄

It's early March when Hernán arrives in the port city. He's out of his element, just as he hoped he'd be, 2,700 kilometers from home. Everything he's brought with him fits in a duffel bag. The university has granted him a one-year leave. Adri has done the same, though she was more open-ended. It is clear that neither really expects him to return.

There is no bus terminal really, just a gravel parking lot at the edge of downtown. Hernán walks the long way into the city, through the narrow, hilly streets. It isn't far, nor is he in a rush. He's heading to the port to look for work, when a door opens. A woman steps from her brightly painted house, wearing a simple dress, so white it glows. Her black hair is pulled back tight. She has a lovely smile, a lovely figure, and stands against a wall as green as the sea, watching him with hands knotted behind her, knowing that she is being admired.

"Excuse me," she says, and this is the story she tells: there's a large pot on an upper shelf that she cannot reach, and she needs it urgently for a dish she's preparing. Hernán is very careful not to smile. It's like a dream he had once. He glances quickly up and down the street. So does she. It's the dead hour just after lunch, and no one else is around.

Hernán drops his duffel by the sofa, and she closes the door behind them. Without a word, she leads him to the kitchen, where there are, in fact, cooking implements on the cramped counter—a cutting board, a knife, four peeled potatoes waiting to be sliced. A pot of water boils languidly on the stove, and various drawers are open. A few flies orbit a rump of beef.

"What are you making?"

"A stew," the woman says. "It will be very tasty."

She fetches Hernán a stepladder, and when he has climbed onto it, reaching blindly to the very top of a cabinet—who would think to hide a pot so high?—he feels her hands on his thighs. He looks down.

"I'm sorry," the woman says. "I was afraid you might fall." She doesn't take her hands away, but bites her lip instead. Her eyelids flutter.

"Where's your husband?"

"At sea. For another six months. He just wrote me."

Her name is Clarisa, she tells him. Years later, a decade from now and even longer, those three syllables will recall for him the shock of this moment, when he stands above her, admiring from this height the curve of her face, the glow of her skin—when he realizes, by the quality of the light streaming in through the window above the sink, that there is much yet to be lived before this day is through.

"It's a beautiful name," Hernán says.

She nods, and then, very slowly, she smiles. "Isn't it?"

A few hours later, he carries his duffel into the bedroom, where the two of them sit, naked, and unpack the few things he has brought with him from his former life. Clarisa empties a drawer for his pants and socks, lays his shirts on the bed and pushes the wrinkles away with the flats of her hands.

"Normally, I wouldn't do this," she says after she has put away his clothes. "But I like you."

"I can see that."

"Under normal circumstances, I'd send you right back out to the street."

"And under normal circumstances, I wouldn't stay."

"But?" Clarisa asks.

He decides to tell the truth: "I have nowhere to go."

That evening, after they've eaten, the dishes rinsed and put away, she asks him where he has come from, and why he is wandering the world alone when he is no longer young. He doesn't answer right away, but wonders how she knows he no longer thinks of himself as young, when only a few weeks before, he had. There is a great deal that he does not want to tell, not now, perhaps not ever.

Clarisa stands and draws the thick curtains so that the room is almost completely dark. She sits back on the bed, but on top of the covers, and there is none of her that touches him. Hernán can tell she will only be satisfied by something that sounds like truth.

He puts his hands on his chest. He closes his eyes, opens them, and there is no difference—darkness binds him on all sides. He takes a deep breath.

✖ APPETITES ✖

When he wakes the next morning, Clarisa gives him keys to the front door and a map. She draws two X's on the map, one for the house, and one for the boutique where she works, a tiny store she co-owns with her friend Lena, where they sell dresses and makeup and overpriced jewelry. "Have fun," she says, and gives Hernán a kiss on the forehead.

He spends the day walking through the sun-splashed streets. If the port town had seen better days, it was nonetheless decaying with a certain dignity. He admires the colorful, crumbling houses, decorated with strips of brightly painted corrugated metal, edges rusting. A sagging clothesline is strung between two apartment blocks, fluttering in the breeze, hanging so low a pant leg brushes him casually along the top of his head as he passes beneath it. He comes upon a pack of teenagers, a gothic, sad-looking bunch, black hair combed down over their eyes, their ears invisible beneath oversize headphones. A boy asks him for cigarettes as he passes—not *a cigarette*, but many, plural—not a hint of innocence in his eyes. Hernán feels very old. He turns to see a woman boarding a bus, carrying her grim, white-haired dog wrapped in a blanket. While she fishes in her pocket for change, she hands the dog to the driver, who accepts the animal without comment.

From certain street corners, Hernán can appreciate the vastness of the sea, so immense it takes his breath away.

Adri and Hernán met when her son, Aurelio, only three at the time, darted away from his mother in the crowded university dining hall and crashed directly into Hernán, who lost his balance and spilled his tray. In spite of everything that had happened since, recalling the story still made him smile. There was a loud crash, and the cafeteria fell momentarily silent. Then: a wailing child, a panicked mother racing to find her boy. Aurelio wasn't hurt, only a little spooked by the collision. Adri was apologetic, but also noticed (couldn't help but notice) the tender way Hernán knelt down to comfort the child, paying no attention to the yogurt and orange juice splattered across his pants and shirt. Her son gazed at this stranger with big, trusting eyes, and in a moment, even before Adri had a chance to comfort him, Aurelio was calm. The bustle of the cafeteria resumed. She offered to replace Hernán's late breakfast, which he chivalrously declined. They ended up eating together anyway.

Now, far away in the port city, Hernán buys a lunch from a stand near the boardwalk, at the edge of a construction site. It's midday and the sun beats down relentlessly; work has slowed. Hernán squints at the artist's rendering of the finished building, regal and elegant, with no apparent relation to the confused cluster of rebar and concrete and wood scaffolding before him. It would require a poet's imagination to intuit a livable structure from the current mess. At one end of the site lies a stack of giant sewer pipes, a dozen or so, and each has a pair of boots poking out from one end. The workers are resting.

That night, when Clarisa returns, they make love, and then she bathes, and then they make love again, until her body is glistening with sweat, and then she falls asleep. "I've been alone too long," she says, as if her desires require explanation or apology. "I'm not usually like this."

"I don't mind," he tells her.

Clarisa has her routines, her customs, and soon she has accommodated him within her ordered world of appetites. If there's nothing else around with which to organize his life, Hernán tells himself, this will do for the time being. After that first night, she never asks him anything—not where he has come from, not what he is fleeing, not what will happen tomorrow or the day after. At some point Clarisa's husband will return, and Hernán will have to leave, but there's no discussion of that now. He feels he has stumbled upon the perfect escape, or fallen prey to some extravagant hoax. When his guard is down, he lets slip a few things: that he taught at a university, for example. "The students called me 'Doctor,'" he adds with a laugh. That he had a wife, and a son.

Most everything else he holds tight. He never says their names aloud.

✖ BINGO ✖

On the fourth day, Hernán finally makes it to the port. To his great disappointment, he's told they're not hiring. The man who informs Hernán of this is not unkind. It's true Hernán has no experience, that he's never worked unloading a ship, but he has read Conrad and Melville and Mutis, has memorized long passages of *The Iliad* and *The Odyssey*, and knows that without the sea and its magnetic call, what we think of as Western civilization simply would not exist. He can't help but feel disappointed, as if by denying him this work the man at the port has robbed him of his rightful inheritance.

Back in the capital, his classes would be starting about

now. He can picture crowded hallways and musty offices, the weary faces of his colleagues. Easiest to conjure are the disheveled students who would be traipsing into his classroom, wiping sleep from their eyes. They are young, privileged, and jaded, genetically engineered to be unimpressed by Hernán or anyone else over thirty. Still, very occasionally, he'd have a breakthrough. He recalls a lecture several years ago, on the relationship between the poetry of the 1930s and the rickety project of nation-building—he'd felt inspired that day, and a few of the students had responded with applause.

With this muted strain of nostalgia swelling his chest, Hernán spends the afternoon looking for a bookstore. He asks a few passersby, and they each smile in that small-town way, either utterly charmed by his question or simply unable to comprehend it, and they point him in different directions—to a newspaper stand, to a stationery store, and finally to a shop at the dark end of an alley, where a ruddy-faced old man pulls the squeaking lever of a mimeograph machine without pause. A worn old fedora hangs from a nail above the light switch, and the old man welcomes Hernán with a nod, unsurprised and unmoved, as if he'd been expecting this visitor. He's producing leaflets for a bingo tournament. On a table to his left, the day's work thus far: a wedding invitation, business cards for a chess teacher, a sign advertising rooms for rent. There is no bookstore in this city, the old man says, unless you count the gift shop of the chapel, which, amid its rosary beads and postcards of obscure saints, also sells copies of the Bible, which is, strictly speaking, a book. "Isn't it?"

The air in the shop is dank, redolent with the pungent, inky smell that the old man has long ago made his peace with. For a moment, Hernán is overwhelmed by it, covers his mouth and nose with his sleeve, coughing into the crook of his elbow.

"Sure," Hernán says when he's recovered. "The Bible is a fine book."

"Are you looking for anything in particular?"

He shakes his head. How can he explain?

"And where are you from?" the mimeographer asks.

"The capital," Hernán says, turning red suddenly, as if he has admitted something shameful.

"The capital, the capital . . ." the old man says once and again, letting the words float around the room. "Never been there."

This he says with a hint of pride.

And then, just like that, he goes back to work, the leaflets appearing one at a time, in an even rhythm, now another, and now another, and so on. His name is Julian, he says, and there's no time to rest. Hernán thanks the old man. He takes the leaflet when it is offered, still warm from the mimeograph machine, and smiles at its blue, sticky ink, its promise of prosperity, implicit in the exclamation point: BINGO!

Out in the street, Hernán's eyes take a moment to adjust to

the light. The sky has begun to shift, filling with purple rain clouds. He folds the scrap of paper into his back pocket, and makes his way back to Clarisa's beneath the darkening sky.

When he arrives, he finds a woman he's never seen before standing in the doorway.

"You must be Hernán," she says.

He nods, because he can't quite think of what else to do.

"It's going to rain soon," she says.

In his pocket, he fingers the keys Clarisa gave him. This time he doesn't answer.

"I'm Lena," she tells him. "Clarisa's friend from the boutique. You're not going to leave me outside in the rain, are you?"

Hernán unlocks the door, and she saunters in, dropping her coat over the back of an armchair before she finds a seat on the sofa. Each of her movements is careful, deliberate, but the sofa doesn't comply with her stagecraft: it's old, gone terribly soft, and she sinks into it like quicksand. "Oh," she says as her feet briefly float above the floor, inelegantly pedaling the air. She rights herself on the unsteady cushion, smiles, and asks for hot tea.

All this happens before Hernán has closed the door.

Hernán sets the water to boil, and when the tea is ready, he joins her. She wears her hair pulled back tightly, the ponytail exploding into a rather unruly knot of curls, her skin the color of milk. She warms her hands against the teacup, bringing it so close to her face that her eyeglasses steam up. She takes them off, lays them on the corner table, and flashes an embarrassed smile, saying nothing.

"Do you live nearby?" Hernán asks.

"Not really.

"Did the shop close early?"

"No," Lena says, after a moment, as though the question required a certain amount of thought. Then: "You're from the capital?"

Hernán nods, sensing she has a question for him but is embarrassed to ask. When she says nothing, he offers: "Have you been there?"

"Sure," she says. "Well, not really."

"Which is it?"

She coughs into her hands. "It doesn't matter, does it?"

It doesn't, he admits, and then they're quiet for a moment. The rains begin, just a pitter-patter on the roof for now.

"Tell me," she says finally, "do you like my teeth?"

"I'm sorry?"

"My teeth. Do you like them?"

Lena spreads her mouth wide open, as if yawning, and bares her gums. Hernán peers into her mouth, taking note of a very ordinary set of teeth. She bites down, and then wiggles her jaw from side to side.

"They seem fine to me."

She takes another sip of tea. "And my eyes?"

"Your eyes."

"How are they?"

He peers at her, squinting even, examining her big green eyes. "No problem there."

"There is the issue of the glasses. I can't see very well without them."

"Yes, there is that."

"But still, I seem to you, in general terms, healthy?"

"I suppose so," says Hernán.

Lena frowns. "You suppose."

He shrugs sheepishly, suddenly wishing he hadn't said anything at all.

"Clarisa said you were a doctor."

He begins to protest, but finds himself unable. Lena's teeth are nearly perfect. Her eyes are a shade of green that recalls a turbid sea. Why get bogged down in details?

"I am," Hernán says. "I'm a doctor."

With that, Lena undoes her ponytail, curls tumbling down to her shoulders. She runs her fingers through them, smiling. Performing. Then she turns away from him, and lifts her hair from the back with her left hand. With her right index finger, she traces a meandering line across the curve of her head, until it comes to rest on a most unexpected bald spot, pink and round, the diameter of a small silver coin.

"Touch it," she says.

And he does: the skin is soft and entirely hairless.

"When did this happen?" he asks, his voice serious, deeper, as he imagines doctors speak when they are concerned.

"I found it two months ago, in the bath." She drops her hair, so that the bald spot is hidden once again behind her curls. "My husband left, and I was worried. I missed him. I thought he'd never come back."

"Has he?"

"Not yet."

Hernán nods. "And how do you feel now?"

She answers with a shrug, and then takes off her sweater. She puts her glasses back on. "I've kept it hidden, and I can't bear to look at it myself. It's important for a woman to have beautiful hair. Clarisa says no one can see it, but I don't believe her. What's it like?"

He reaches for the back of her head, searching. Her hair is so thick, it seems impossible the spot can be hidden there. "Turn around," Hernán says, and she does.

The rain is falling heavily now. What a sound! Hernán imagines an entire concert hall roaring in appreciation, and it's all he can do to not stand up and take a bow. He scans the room, empty but for the two of them, swollen with noise. And maybe this explains it, Hernán thinks: why when she turns her back to him and settles into the couch—why when she leans her head forward into her chest and he runs his hand up her neck to examine the bald spot—why he feels as if he is onstage, that there are thousands of people in Clarisa's home, all watching, wondering, waiting to see what he will do next. In truth, he's wondering too, watching his hands—their greedy movements—as if they belong to someone else. Lena's neck is very beautiful, and he sits close to her as she takes deep, steady breaths, her shoulders rising gently. He uses both hands to find the bald spot, kneading her head as he searches, and she moans very softly. When he finds it, he parts her brown curls, and once again examines the pink clearing. So small and sad. He bends closer to the back of her head, and kisses it. She doesn't stop him, and so he does it again, and then to her neck, and then just below.

The rain announces its approval.

▰ CONFESSIONS ▰

When she has gone, Hernán tidies the house, trying to understand what he feels. A little confused, a little ashamed. Physically, quite content, full of a recognizably adolescent sort of pride. He finds the scrap of paper the old man gave him stuffed between the cushions. *Bingo!* he reads, and wonders exactly what he's won. These are not the sorts of things that happen to him. Lena has gone, the tidy home restored to its original appearance, and Hernán is simply bewildered. If only there was someone he could brag to, or commiserate with, he thinks, but of course, there isn't, not here, not even back home in the city. No one would believe him. No one would care. It's for the best, naturally. A gentleman never tells, etc., etc. He wonders what these women want from him, and what it is about this town that has made him so irresistible.

Is it the salty sea air?

More likely: The fact that half the men are at sea?

Or is it simply better not to question these things?

He lies down on the couch, meaning only to rest a moment, but when he wakes it is dark, and Clarisa is home, quietly making dinner. She hears him shift on the sofa, and moves toward him, visible only in silhouette, framed by the light of the kitchen.

"How was your day?" she asks brightly.

✜ CIRCLES ✜

When he met Adri, she was a graduate student in biology, recently divorced, balancing single motherhood with the challenges of work. She handled it well for the most part—Aurelio's father was only an occasional presence—but much later she confessed how hard she'd worked at first to make it all seem effortless. That's what's demanded of women, isn't it? Hernán hadn't been exactly unaware, just unable to process it all: he saw her feed the boy, bathe him, play with him, sing to him, read to him, put him to sleep. But what he didn't (couldn't) understand was precisely how much energy it required to do those things, do them well, and then take a deep breath and stroll from the dark bedroom, where the child slept, and into her living room, where Hernán was waiting. He didn't (couldn't) understand how hard it was to be fresh again, renewed, funny, attractive. He was falling in love, in the profoundly selfish way men often do. He wanted her for himself.

Still, the most ordinary details about your new partner's life can feel like fascinating, otherworldly discoveries—Hernán was pleased, for example, to find Adri so entertained by his stories of the drab suburb where he'd been raised. He'd describe his mother, a strong, coolly competent physician's assistant, always on time in a country where punctuality was considered a sign of weakness, and Adri would shake her head in recognition and admiration. For her part, she would tell him what it was like being the pretty, lower-middle-class girl at the fancy upper-class private school, evoking in great detail the tedious gaggle of privileged boys in pastel sweaters who lined up to impress her with their wealth. Hernán guffawed at her descriptions of these would-be Romeos, interpreting her rejection of the suitors as a subtle kind of class war.

It helped that neither knew much about the other's field of study—they embarked on a project of mutual education, which not only served as the basis of their engagement, but also reminded each of them how much they enjoyed their work. Hernán was becoming an expert in the nation's most obscure modernist poets; Adri, almost by osmosis, was too. She was studying the biology of drought-resistant crops; Hernán became, for a time, nominally conversant with the coping mechanisms of various edible plants.

This is where they began, and it wasn't so long ago.

Meanwhile, the boy was a three-year-old chatterbox, clumsy, strong-willed, fearless. The first time Hernán visited the apartment where they lived, Aurelio took him by the hand, and showed him the hallway: the white walls were adorned with long colorful streaks of crayon. "Snakes," he said. "I drew them." A few steps farther, he stopped in front of a mess of scribbled circles, one atop the other. "Spaghetti," he said. He was outgoing, unafraid. Nothing in Hernán's study of poetics had prepared him for the improbable beauty of the boy's emerging syntax. His sentences were consistently more inventive than three quarters of the chapbooks on Hernán's shelf. He recited the alphabet with the seriousness befitting a speech before parliament. He hid his favorite toys, as if someone might take them away, and no matter how obscure the hiding place, never forgot them, not once. It hadn't occurred to Hernán that a child so young could have so much personality. Sometimes he'd wake up with the boy sitting on his chest, a wild smile across his lips, and Hernán would wonder what he'd done to deserve such good fortune.

It wasn't long before Hernán had moved in.

But the years passed, and inevitably, they were not that trio of strangers anymore, marveling at their luck; they were a family, with all the intimacy and anxiety that word implies. He hadn't finished his dissertation, and until he did, his teaching career was stalled. Adri, more driven, more responsible, had managed to graduate, and found work teaching at a private high school. The pay was decent, but predictably enough, Hernán and Adri fought about money. They fought about Aurelio, about her ex. The winters were particularly difficult. The city felt oppressive.

When he was six, Aurelio ran away—or so they thought for four frantic hours, until the police found him, knees pressed to his chest, hidden behind a suitcase in the farthest corner of the utility closet. Volunteers were already combing the neighborhood, but they were called off, everyone relieved and a little annoyed, while Adri and Hernán were simply embarrassed to have caused such a commotion. They were furious with the boy, but also grateful to have him back (though he'd never left). Privately, they were impressed that he'd stayed so quiet, so still, for so long. Of course, that too was concerning.

And the more their relationship shifted, the better they got at telling their story of love at first sight. It became the sort of moment that felt choreographed by a team of sitcom writers. At a dinner party, in front of friends and strangers, around a long table dotted with empty wine bottles and full ashtrays and dirty plates waiting to be cleared, they'd be asked, and inevitably, their origin story was met with a warm, collective sigh. Often, the boy himself was present for the telling, older now, sitting on his stepfather's lap, ready to offer commentary on the charming scene his parents were relating. "I don't remember that," he might say. Or: "They're making it up." Or: "I ran into him on purpose." The sort of observations that only made the anecdote more touching.

Hernán and Adri knew when their audience would laugh, when they'd express disbelief; knew when one should interrupt the other and take over the telling for maximum effect. The lunch tray no longer fell to the floor—it *twisted* through the air, its contents *raining down on the cowering child like shrapnel*. The orange juice no longer splashed on Hernán's pants, it *soaked* them, *drenched* them. It was a *flood*. His shirt became *a Jackson Pollock of yogurt*.

None of it was untrue per se, only magnified. It had become a story they told to reassure themselves.

And then there came a time when they no longer told it at all, when the disconnect between the nostalgia of the story and the daily reality of their relationship had become too much to ignore.

✖ A PIGEON BURNS ✖

Hernán finds work busing tables at the Versailles, a restaurant not far from Clarisa's boutique, a relic from the city's more prosperous days, a large, light-filled room with high ceilings and ornate chandeliers, its walls adorned with bucolic paintings of mountain sunsets, or nostalgic depictions of nineteenth-century battles, when death was still an elegant, even aristocratic, sacrifice to offer the young nation. There's a long wooden bar in need of a polish, but its stately bearing recalls the dining room of an old transoceanic cruise ship. When the restaurant is full, bursting with noise and conversation and laughter, when Hernán is rushing from table to crowded table, he can almost feel the room tilt, as if on a gently rolling sea.

The pay is indecent. The manager is a little man named Holden, who fills his black suit nearly to bursting, and leads the team of waiters and cooks and busboys with a schizophrenic unpredictability. Gentle and generous in the morning, lunchtime might find him handing out insults with the depraved smile of a carnival barker. On the fourth afternoon, after the last client has been served, Holden gathers his staff and lists all the day's errors, recalling for everyone the Versailles's prestigious past, its traditions. The workers stand awkwardly, pretending to listen and waiting to be excused, as

Holden lists a few historical figures of dubious significance who have dined at the restaurant over the course of its one hundred twenty years of uninterrupted service. Hernán is caught by surprise when one of the men—and naturally, all historical figures are men—is Carlos Max, the poet whose abbreviated oeuvre Hernán studied for his unfinished dissertation. He smiles in spite of himself—so odd that his former life would appear in such a place—and Holden interprets the smile as disrespect, so he explodes. The rest of the staff relaxes slightly—Hernán can sense it; they are relieved that Holden has chosen his target for the day, that they have each been spared. Not that Hernán minds. Next time it will be someone else, and so for now he enjoys the spectacle: the manager's face is lined with a complex latticework of wrinkles, age heaped upon age, and as he shouts all of him reddens, even the skin beneath his thinning white hair. Hernán wonders if Holden has served in the restaurant since its halcyon days, back when the rich people of the port city still imagined they were descended from the Spanish, the French, and the English, and women struggled into petticoats as a matter of routine.

As he daydreams, the moment ends.

One day, there's a fire across the street. Hernán and the rest of the staff and the buttoned-up lunchtime crowd gather on the sidewalk to watch the flames consume the top floor of the three-story building. It burns like a Roman candle, bright against the noonday sky. A tenant had kept a pigeon coop on the roof, and as the flames rise, the air is heavy with the shrill hysterics of a dozen trapped and desperately squawking birds. Traffic stops, and people pour into the streets to get a better look, while the city's beleaguered company of volunteer firemen briefly amuse the blaze with a feeble plume of water. There's very little left of the top floor, everything hidden by thick gray smoke, when a few pigeons finally escape. Part of the cage must have tumbled, or the mesh melted in the heat, and suddenly a handful of birds rise from the burning rooftop, and the gathered crowd sighs with relief. Then they catch sight of it, all at once: a pigeon, the last to emerge, aflame; its burning wings flail helplessly for an instant before it falls. "Aahhh," says the crowd in a single, despairing voice. The remaining pigeons make a frantic loop around the fallen bird before disappearing in the direction of the sea.

The restaurant closes for the afternoon, and as Hernán walks home, blocks from the fire, he is surprised to feel a fine, ashen mist float down upon him. He holds his tongue out; he tastes it. The gray-white ash coats the windows of the cars parked along the street, settles into the cracks in the sidewalk. With his index finger, he writes his name in a dusted car window. He likes the way it looks, and so he writes it again, and then a few others. Aurelio's. Adri's. The man he suspects may be sleeping with Adri now that he's gone. (Not that he blames her for that.) He writes Clarisa's name too. Not Lena's, of course. The street is empty but for these ghosts, abruptly and needlessly conjured, and a yellow-eyed cat, skittering along the wall beside him.

That night he mentions the fire to Clarisa. Already, she is drifting toward sleep.

"There's a fire every week," she says. "You'll get used to it."

He considers this, considers how much he enjoyed the quiet, powdery snowfall, the remains of the incinerated building that had so unexpectedly sprinkled his clothes and his hair and his tongue as he made his way home. He'd had no thought of the dead, injured, or displaced, only the pleasures of the spectacle and this ashy mist. Suddenly, belatedly, he feels concern, then guilt.

"Every week? Someone should do something."

"All the time," she murmurs, and a moment later is asleep.

❧ DOCTOR ❧

He's walking home from the Versailles one day when he feels certain he's being followed. It's hard to say how he knows, but he *knows*. If this were a movie, he thinks, the background music would be tense and ominous. At every corner, he looks over his shoulder to scan the street and the crowded sidewalk behind him, but he sees only strangers. He feels silly.

Farther up the hill, away from the center of town, everything slows, and that's when he sees her. He was right after all.

"I'm Cristina," she tells him, and confesses that she's been five or ten paces behind him for blocks now. She laughs nervously.

"Are you heading to Clarisa's?" she asks. "Oh, of course you are."

"She's at work."

Cristina shakes her head. "No, she told me to come by."

He looks her over: smiling awkwardly, wearing a not-quite-flattering yellow dress, trimmed with white. She has long, straight black hair and a leather bag over her shoulder that looks too heavy for her. Her dark eyes lock on to his, and Hernán is unwilling to argue. He offers to carry her bag for her, but she demurs.

They head off together.

Cristina, he notices a few blocks on, walks with a limp—a slight, barely noticeable imperfection to her gait, but now, side by side, he can *hear* it in the rhythm of her feet against the pavement. He's listening for it very carefully when she says, "I've known Clarisa since we were girls."

A bus stops at the corner, exhaling a cloud of students in gray-and-white uniforms. Hernán and Cristina watch them scatter.

"Since we were that age," she adds.

Hernán doesn't answer.

Clarisa is not, in fact, at home, but Cristina invites herself in anyway, and once inside, she sits at the kitchen table, and opens her bag to reveal a stack of papers wrapped in a rubber band. She places it on the table, then hangs the bag on the back of her wooden chair, where she sits upright, eager, full of anticipation.

"What's this?" Hernán asks.

"My records." She removes the rubber band with a long, delicate finger. "Clarisa said you were a doctor."

It seems suddenly cruel to pretend he isn't. He takes a deep breath.

"Of course."

Cristina smiles and fans her papers on the table, X-rays and charts and diagrams and wrinkled, old prescriptions. "Pick one, any one," she says, as if it were a card trick. "You know this game."

CHANGE

By his second week at the Versailles, they have a new routine: on days when he's scheduled to start early, Hernán walks with Clarisa into the center of town. They don't hold hands as they stroll, and he's grateful for this; content to walk alongside her, breathing in the clean, brisk smell of the damp city. He's become accustomed to her; and she to him, he hopes. At times he thinks he might be happy, though he isn't, of course, not really.

The weather has shifted, the rains more frequent now,

and every morning the sidewalks are slick. Pools of muddy water gather in the places where the cobblestone is broken. The street dogs shake off the wet, and commence their scavenging with more than the usual urgency. Down in the flats, where the rain has overwhelmed the sewers, the cars move slowly, bald tires breaking the oily skin of the water, spreading tiny wakes as they pass. The sun is dazzling, unexpected surfaces reflecting light, and at certain angles, the city seems to be made of silver. It's all very beautiful, Hernán thinks, much more than he'd expected, or had a right to expect when he stepped on the night bus headed away from the capital.

Usually Clarisa leaves him at the door of the restaurant, and walks the few blocks to the boutique on her own, but one morning, they're lost in conversation when he realizes they've passed the Versailles, and are heading to the boutique instead. He feels a knot of panic in his chest. His two liaisons with Clarisa's friends have left him unsettled. He looks for the women everywhere. He has no practical experience with infidelity, and his discomfort, he feels certain, will be visible to any and all. He was never very good at secrets.

But when they get to the shop, Lena hasn't come yet—relief! He can escape!—and while Clarisa rummages through her bag for her keys, Hernán does his best not to fidget. She's in no rush, chatty and content, half an arm buried in a bag so oversize Hernán might, under slightly different circumstances, find it comical. It would be quicker to spill every-thing onto the sidewalk, he thinks. Finally, she declares that she must've left the keys at home.

"So we wait," she adds, in a voice that accepts no dissent. Hernán wants at all costs to leave before Lena arrives. He checks his watch, and is beginning to say that he must be going when suddenly—she's there.

"The famous Hernán!" Lena says. She's wearing a blue dress and simple leather sandals. Her hair is just as it was when she walked in that day, pulled back tight, the same bloom of curls emerging from the ponytail, and in spite of himself, he's searching for it, that tiny hairless spot hidden beneath.

"Don't be shy!" says Clarisa to Hernán.

Both women chuckle.

"It's wonderful to meet you," Lena says.

He can feel himself blush. Clarisa makes the formal intro-ductions, and they exchange a polite kiss on the cheek, Hernán suddenly demure, careful not to make actual contact with her skin. *I'm panicking,* he thinks, and feels shame wash over him. Surely Lena noticed that I didn't kiss her; surely she took it as an insult.

Back in the real world, a conversation is under way: "Clarisa tells me you have a new job."

"I do."

Hernán gazes down the street, squinting against the sun, which has made the blacktop a slick runway of pure light.

"And?"

Clarisa answers for him. "He hates it, naturally."

"I do?"

"Of course you do, sweetie," Clarisa says. "You're not made for that sort of place. Terrible people there. Ordinary people." She turns to Lena. "He's a doctor, remember."

"Oh, yes, that's right," Lena says. She bites her lip. "Tell me, Hernán: What's your specialty?"

They laugh before he can answer. Hernán wonders why they're so happy.

▰ TODAY'S THEME IS REGRET ▰

It's true they were shaken when Aurelio ran away. Anyone would've been. But they quickly decided it had been an isolated incident, an anxiety-inducing but ultimately discrete moment that augured nothing. Everything went back to normal.

The boy mostly cooperated. He continued hiding his toys beneath sofa cushions, behind doors, inside low cabinets around the apartment. He continued dancing down the hallway in his socks every morning, and spending an eternity selecting a stuffed animal to accompany him to preschool each day. (Every morning, Rabbit, Cow, and Fox were brought to the sofa, arranged like suspects to be interrogated or contestants in some kind of game show, summoned to argue their cases before the tiny boy-judge.)

Every weekday morning, Hernán walked Aurelio to preschool, about ten blocks from the apartment, across the park and just beyond the avenue they'd nicknamed "the River," for its constant flow of cars and buses, and because it was, in fact, named after the country's longest river, a multisyllabic indigenous name the boy found difficult to pronounce. When it rained, the gutters swelled, channels of churning water forming at the sidewalk's edge; these were Aurelio's favorite days, when the imaginary river became a real one. On those occasions, Hernán had to pick the boy up and carry him across, so insistent was the child on his right to wade into the dark puddles and ruin his sneakers.

They were crossing the River one morning, a few months after Aurelio's brief disappearance, when the boy said, "This is where I wanted to come. That day. This is where I was headed."

"When?"

"The day I ran away."

They still talked about it as "running away," even though, strictly speaking, he'd never left the apartment. The panic of it came rushing back, and suddenly the traffic of the River felt impossibly dense. Hernán shut his eyes for a moment, the sun on his face. He felt the swirl of light behind his eyes and took a deep breath.

"Why would you want to come here?"

"Because it's so loud," the boy said. "If I'm here, I can just listen. I don't think at all. I can just listen."

Hernán gripped Aurelio's hand tightly. Until recently, maybe a year ago, he'd always lifted the boy when crossing the River. He was so afraid Aurelio might slip from his grasp, and drivers in this city were animals. It was Adri who'd finally put an end to it: no, she said, the boy was old enough to cross the street by himself. He had to learn to be more independent.

"Why do you like it so loud?" Hernán asked.

"So I don't have to hear you fighting with Mami."

Fighting sounded so coarse. Hernán wouldn't have used that word. If he was describing the conversation he was having with Adri that day, he might've said they were *disagreeing loudly*. He felt the blood rushing to his cheeks; the traffic slowed for a light, and they stepped into the River. Hernán knew he should say something—a word of assurance so the boy wouldn't worry—but he was worried himself. He'd tell Adri about this, he resolved. He'd tell her what the boy had said, which was, in a way, good news. If we can fix this, he won't run away again. So easy! He'd tell her, and they'd promise things would get better, for Aurelio, for themselves.

But he didn't get the chance. That night his evening class

ran late, and by the time he made it home, Adri and Aurelio were asleep. It was just as well. He was tired too.

▰ ANOTHER MAN'S MONEY ▰

At the end of each week, he brings his paycheck home to Clarisa, though she hasn't asked for it. She accepts it without comment.

Clarisa's husband, Josué, sends letters twice a month, penned in a shaky script only she can decipher. She reads them aloud to Hernán sometimes, as if to remind him she is not the kind of woman her liaisons might imply. Occasionally the sailor strikes upon a nice turn of phrase, a poetic description of his work, or a sentence that evokes something of the loneliness one must confront when there is nothing for the eye to seize upon but endless water. Part of Hernán is even jealous. The wandering husband wires money whenever he arrives in port, not much, but the modest amounts do allow Hernán and Clarisa certain comforts. For her part, Clarisa never complains about working. The hours pass quickly at the boutique, she tells Hernán. She and Lena have been friends since they were girls. Most of the customers are friends too, women with whom Clarisa says she has no secrets.

Hernán says nothing, though he feels certain this isn't true.

He makes a point of taking early shifts, so as to avoid the

complication of running into Lena. Instead he leaves just as the sun is rising, when Clarisa is still asleep, and one morning his legs feel heavy, so he decides to take the bus into the center of town. This is hardly a time-saving proposition, Hernán realizes as the bus climbs farther and farther into the hills, carving a byzantine route away from the center of the city. The bus finally makes it to the ridge, and the bay is spread out before them, wide and gleaming, the city center visible too, a handful of buildings rising above the rest, more lovely at this distance than they are up close. The bus speeds along now, slowing occasionally to pick up a few students, or a maid in her pristine white uniform, or a working man, heading to the port with a cheap newspaper under his arm. "Right foot, right foot," the driver mutters when Hernán is getting off, but the advice doesn't register. He steps with his left from the moving bus, and just like that, his ankle twists, and pain shrieks up his leg.

He limps the rest of the way to the restaurant.

That afternoon, when the Versailles has emptied, Hernán takes a cab to the house he has come to think of as his home. In the backseat, he pulls up his pant leg and examines his ankle; what he finds is a swirl of purple and blue, shades of a stormy sea, a blending of colors he might consider beautiful were it not for the pain. He takes a deep breath, and directs the driver to Clarisa's house. There, he pulls himself gingerly from the car, and once inside, he takes four aspirin and two glasses of whiskey before limping to bed. Clarisa finds him there, a few hours later, sleeping with his shirt off and his mouth agape.

He tells her everything.

"You poor thing," Clarisa murmurs. She's wearing a white dress—the one she wore when they first met—and drifts in and out of the room with the grace of a dancer. "I'm listening," she calls as she flits through the small house, and it's the first time he's complained about work to her. She brings him another drink, and sits by his bedside, placing a gentle hand over his eyes. She lays a bag of ice on his ankle. Then she tells him to quit the Versailles.

"What about money?"

She shrugs, as if the thought hadn't occurred to her. "We have money."

Her blithe use of the plural pronoun is startling.

"*His* money, you mean."

"What's the difference?"

"Well . . ."

"Quit," she says again. "Make a scene. I want to see you do it. What's his name? Your manager?"

"Holden."

"Hurt him."

"Do you know him?"

"I know everyone in this fucking town," she says. "And I hate them all."

It's impossible to argue with her.

Clarisa smiles. The light is low, and she takes a deep breath. "Now," she says, "pretend you are very ill. Pretend you've washed up in some faraway hospital, a shell of a man."

It's what he's been doing for hours.

Clarisa wraps a bandage around his head, covering his eyes, and tears the pants off him. His ankle throbs, but she removes the ice. "Listen," she says. "There's no pain anymore. Only silence. It's the end of the war."

"Which war?"

"Any war. It was terrible. It was bloody. You saw awful things. Men decapitated. Entire villages burned. Your heart is broken, but you survived, only you can't think of any reason why this should be taken as good news. You and your men are holed up near the northern border."

"I'm a lieutenant?"

"Sure. Or a colonel, or whatever is higher. You're in charge. There are refugees crowding the roads to the capital, leaving with whatever they can carry, and walking south. Everyone fleeing. Maybe a peace has been signed, maybe it hasn't. There's been no news for weeks, only the steady rumble of artillery fire, and planes sailing overhead."

"Planes!"

"You've been told to stay and fight to the last man, but in

your heart of hearts, you don't want to die just yet. You see the faces of your soldiers, their tired, ragged faces, and think, 'This is just too much.' They're children. Conscripts from poor northern villages, a bunch of ignorant, illiterate teenagers who've never lived. Probably all virgins. They've never seen a map in their entire lives, and have no idea why they're fighting. An enemy attack is imminent. Your supply lines are weak. You stay up all night, praying, and then you make your decision. You don't want their deaths on your conscience. For what? This war is stupid. You will be vilified, called a deserter and worse. You know it, but you don't care. The next morning, you order your men to break camp. 'We're going south,' you say. 'We're retreating?' the soldiers ask. 'We can't do that.' You shake your head. You clarify—'We're not *retreating*, we're going south.' 'But we can't,' they say."

"They don't want to go?"

"Of course not. They're young and they're foolish and they don't know the first thing about death."

"And I do."

"Sure you do. Your wife and child were killed in a bombing raid."

"They were," Hernán says, his voice just above a whisper.

"As far as you're concerned, you're already dead. It's all the same to you. It was these young boys you were thinking of, but if they want to stay and die, who are you to stop them? 'We'll stay,' you announce. They raise a cheer. A reckless, suicidal cheer. Then the attack comes, and it's worse than you thought. Wave after wave of bombing, thousands of enemy soldiers, hordes of them, pouring over the horizon thick as ants, and these children around you, these lightly armed boys, they step in front of bullets, as they were trained to do, and die one after another, and all you can think of is your son."

"How old was he?"

"Young. Ten or eleven. He wrote you letters about what he was learning in school. About a blond-haired girl he liked. About a Ferris wheel set up at the edge of town, how his mother wouldn't let him ride it. Dangerous, she said. And then the letters stopped coming. No one had to tell you what happened. And in the battle, you think of these letters, and your son, and you order your men to lay down their arms. 'Give up, damn it!' you scream. There's no point anymore. This time, the ones who've survived, they're afraid, and they listen to you, of course. The battlefield is strewn with the bodies of their comrades. All these lives you could've saved, the dead who perished with their eyes open, dreaming of glory. You are taken prisoner. And though you have no injuries, you are unable to move. Unable to speak. Bedridden. You stare at the wall all day long. The enemy thinks you're faking, but it's not that at all. You have injuries *no one can see*."

"They think I'm a coward."

"But I don't."

"And who are you?"

"I'm an enemy nurse with a young boy, and I hate the war. I've lost my husband. You remind me of him. You're the same age. I wouldn't understand your language, even if you spoke. But I think you're beautiful."

"Really?" Hernán feels her nails tracing lines on the insides of his legs. "And so?"

"So," Clarisa says. "I decide to cure you."

✄ THE BATTLE ✄

Clarisa arranges to be at the Versailles the next day, so she can see him quit. She's made him promise a show, and he has, though he's not really certain what that means. He's dressing in the break room, when another busser says that Holden wants to see him.

Holden has a tiny office in the back, with a grease-stained window facing the kitchen. He's examining a ledger when Hernán walks in. He doesn't say anything, just looks up with his little eyes, tapping his fingers against the desk. He probably sleeps back here, Hernán thinks.

"Are you all right?" Holden asks.

"What do you mean?"

Holden sighs. "You were slow yesterday. A few customers complained."

The office wall is cluttered with cheaply framed photos of

local soccer teams, parade floats, and the like. There is one image of a sinking ship, tilting hopelessly toward the sky, and another of a family on a pier, with the same ship in the distance, its nose nearly perpendicular to the horizon. It is a windy day. Everyone is cheerful, pointing at the disaster and smiling, except the father, who wears dark glasses and a stern impression that could be Holden's.

"Your family?" Hernán asks, nodding at the picture.

Holden softens, offering a smile so unexpected, so obscure, Hernán is briefly alarmed.

"They were here when I took over. Thirty-two years ago." He pauses. "My sons are grown now. Those aren't them, but I guess I never took the pictures down."

Hernán is waiting for more, but the manager shrugs. That's all there is, so Hernán lifts up his left leg, resting his heel on the desk. He pulls up the fabric of his pressed gray pants to reveal the splotchy skin around his ankle. "I couldn't walk. Barely stand."

Holden nods. "I see. And today?"

"Better."

"Can you work?"

Hernán wonders for a moment if he's being sent home, today of all days. "Yes," he says.

"Okay. So do your best."

"Excuse me?"

"Your best," the manager says. "That's all. Maybe it'll be a quiet day. Anything else?"

"Did the poet Carlos Max really eat here?"

Holden frowns. "Who?"

"You mentioned him in your speech the other day."

The manager waves a disinterested hand in the air. "How should I know?"

The day is busy, like any other, and his ankle really does hurt. Hernán thinks of the soldier he became last night. The battle he survived and the promise he made. The memory carries him through the morning, until the lunchtime crowd rushes in, among them Clarisa with two friends. Lena is one of them; the other he's never seen before. They're seated at a table in the center of the dining room, the three of them watching Hernán carefully as he maneuvers through the restaurant, carrying his tub of dirty dishes. His hands are cold and damp, his apron mostly clean. He can feel their anticipation. He spots Holden across the dining room, and the manager smiles at him.

Hernán wonders: *What am I doing?*

At the height of lunch hour, Holden tends to glide back and forth along a straight line that runs from the entrance to the end of the waiter station at one end of the bar, very rarely stepping out among the diners, unless to greet a table and shake hands with one of the sharp-suited, silver-haired gentlemen who run the city and its port. Mostly he keeps watch, surveying the floor like a general, occasionally giving an order in the gruff, unaffectionate tone reserved most often for a misbehaving pet. There is something quixotic about Holden's quest for perfection. A mistake-free lunchtime rush—it must be what Holden dreams of.

Later, he'll admit it: the fact that Holden had done nothing to deserve what's coming is all the more satisfying. *Maybe,* Hernán thinks, *this is what I've needed all along. A capacity for malice. A mean streak. Didn't my father always tell me this? Didn't he have it, and my grandfather before him? Why not me?*

Hernán steals a glance at Clarisa, at her friends, who pick at their meals, daintily, without much enthusiasm because after all, they have not come to eat, but to be entertained. Hernán lets it happen. He counts to ten. Little by little, the room begins to sway, the soothing ebb and flow of the sea, and Hernán must remind himself to breathe. He is sure this is happening, but is it happening to him? He approaches Holden, who turns just in time, no idea what awaits him. Hernán doesn't smile—he's too far beyond that now—instead, with one swift motion, he takes his gray plastic tub and swings it against Holden's head. The old man crumples to the floor.

It's awful, so unnecessary and magnificent. Hernán can hardly believe the joy he feels.

The dining room goes quiet, just as it had when Aurelio ran into him so many years ago. Hernán beats the manager with his plastic tub, not savagely, but efficiently, to the rhythm of his breath. He catches a thought as it flits across his fevered brain: *Why don't I do this more often?* The beating goes on for a euphoric, senseless minute, and to his surprise there is no resistance. No one intervenes. Holden barely manages to cover his face. He whimpers.

Finally, Hernán feels a hand on his shoulder. Clarisa.

"That's enough," she whispers. "You were wonderful."

Hernán takes off his apron, drops it on the floor beside Holden, and walks out. He doesn't look back.

⊯ THE MUSEUM ⊯

He spends his first morning without work worrying, peeking through the curtains at the empty street. He drinks his coffee, half expecting the police to burst in at any moment and arrest him, but Clarisa has assured him this won't happen. The city is too disorganized for that, and people are beaten in public all the time, she says. He's never seen such violence, nor is it comforting to learn that he has made a home, even a temporary one, in such a place. Still, some facts are on his side: no one at the restaurant ever bothered to get his full name, or his address. He never signed any papers, and was always paid in cash. It's not as if Holden is dead. According to Clarisa, he sat up only a few minutes after Hernán fled ("'Fled'? Is that the right word? Didn't I just *walk out*?"), groggy, bruised, but alive.

Still, Hernán is uneasy. It's late April, six weeks since he left the city, nearly four months since he left the apartment he'd shared with Adri. Sometimes it's the middle of the afternoon before he's really thought about how he arrived here, while on other mornings, he wakes with Aurelio's name on his lips, and shame like a vise gripping his chest. He has nothing to do, so he decides to write a letter.

Dear Aurelio, he writes, *Welcome to the museum of my new life,* and he goes on to describe the small, comfortable home that he shares with Clarisa (*as pretty as your mother,* he might have written . . .), the unwitting generosity of her seafaring husband, who is due home in five months, and the charms of a city where buildings burn with startling regularity. Besides that first fire, there have been three others—smaller, less spectacular—and a day of mourning for the first anniversary of a gas explosion that claimed a half-dozen lives. But none of it really registers. The city exists in a kind of stupor. The bay is undeniably beautiful, and the clouds, when they come, are high, white ornaments, like the ribbon adorning a woman's Sunday hat. And yet: the children all wear black and never let anyone see them smile. At night they wander the alleys and write their names on the old city walls with thick black markers. The elderly shoo them away by name, as they do the street dogs, as important to the city as any human resident, more important than many. The port is the only place that stays open late; in fact, it never closes, and its constant clang and hiss is the town's true lifeblood. But only ten blocks away, everything is quiet, and every night the fog rolls in, impossibly heavy, so an evening stroll is like walking backward in time, into a living gallery of diffuse, grainy photographs. On every corner, a yellow street lamp scatters its weak light, illuminating nothing, and the moisture simply hangs in the air, never appearing to rise or fall. In the bars along the main avenue, the bent old men gather to tell stories of their youths misspent at sea. By noon the next day, the sun shines mercilessly, relentlessly, and everything is dry, so that in truth, there are two versions of this place, one burning and parched, one rotting and damp. Or perhaps there are more than two, and these are simply the ones he has discovered thus far. Perhaps he will leave before he stumbles onto a third version. (Though where would he go?)

Hernán finds the place difficult to describe, but he does what he can, while the story of the restaurant and his run-in with Holden—this comes easily. A confession. *I have beaten a man,* Hernán writes, *a man as old as my own father,* and when he sees these words on the page, Hernán feels ashamed. He describes Holden's bright red face frozen in shock. *I am unemployed now,* he writes, and this feels strangest of all. He's worked since he was his stepson's age, first in his father's furniture shop, as his old man's mistreated and consistently disappointing assistant; then, when he confessed to his father that he wanted to be paid, for the neighborhood grocery store, where he swept the concrete floors with a wood-handled broom taller than he was. "Like dancing," the grocer told him with a flourish. Later, when he began his studies at the university, he collected tickets at the central train station, an art deco monstrosity long since shuttered, scheduled for demolition any day now. There were flocks of bats sleeping up in the rafters, and they would wake at dusk, as the late train from the north pulled in, and swoop down low over the arriving passengers' heads. It was a wonderful job. He spent most of the day reading—and now? He hasn't picked up a book in weeks. His brain is atrophying. *There is no need to work now,* he writes. *There is no need to do anything. Josué sends money enough for the both of us.*

When he's finished his letter, he folds the thin pages into an envelope. *Now what?* he asks himself. What does an unemployed man do in a city like this? He has seen them—the old and infirm, and the others, much too young to be doing nothing, those men who shuffle down the streets, and sit for long hours on park benches in the shade, spending all day reading a single page from a poorly written newspaper. They feed the pigeons. They play checkers with colored stones in place of pieces lost long ago. They speak indecently to the women who happen by, and otherwise communicate among themselves in an invented language of gestures and nonsense words. Will that be his life now? *Will I die here?*

Back in the capital, Hernán had lived with Adri and Aurelio in an apartment overlooking a park. A nice enough place, though not large. The apartment's best feature was its balcony, which on a breezy day was a fine place to take in the scent of eucalyptus and stare at the clouds as they drifted indolently across the sky. It was on the second floor, so that its view of the park was somewhat obscured by a stand of leafy trees on the near sidewalk. When Aurelio was three or four, Hernán would sit on this balcony, the boy on his knee, and together they would talk about the park as if it were a faraway land, completely foreign and unlike the grounds they walked through several times a week. The boy had a magical imagination. The park had waterfalls, secret tunnels burrowed in the earth, flocks of exotic birds. It had been one of the boy's favorite games—this reimagining—and his ability to play without distraction was one of those attributes Hernán felt the child had inherited from him. Of course, the boy had not, strictly speaking, inherited anything from him, not genetically, only learned it, but did that really make a difference? By the time Hernán moved out of the apartment, they hadn't played this game in years.

And this is what Hernán thinks that afternoon as he's finishing his letter: One day, when Aurelio is older, no longer a child, he will come upon the park of his youth again. He will be an adult, perhaps a student at the university, and he will be driving to pick up a girlfriend, say, or a young woman he is only beginning to know, but whose smile he finds captivating. Her eyes will be brown or green. She will give him an address, a time, a coquettish look, and he will arrive in a borrowed car, which he has washed himself for this very occasion. He won't notice that the address is so close to the place where he once lived, because in truth, he hasn't thought of it in a very long time. He arrives, he checks his watch, he realizes he has come early. He'll drive around to a side street, and turn off the car. A few minutes to kill. Into the park then, where it will hit him slowly: this curving cobblestone path, that fountain, these sagging benches, those eucalyptus trees with their scent of imminent rain. How long has it been? Then he'll recall the exotic birds, the system of tunnels he'd once imagined with that man who was his stepfather, the electric rivers and glass-bottomed boats, the goblins he'd decided lived here after dark, the music they made when no one else was around. He'll remember Hernán—his sad face, his dark hair, his sad eyes. Aurelio will walk around the park, stunned and silent, a young man losing himself. A bank of fog will settle over the city, then night will come, and still Hernán's son (no longer his son) will be there. Morning will come, and noon too, and when the fog has lifted, when the sun is out, an old woman out walking her dog will find the boy, asleep on a bench and dreaming.

⬛ AN INTERRUPTION ⬛

He's finishing the letter when there's a knock at the door. It's the other woman, the one who'd sat with Lena and Clarisa at the Versailles.

She stands expectantly in the middle of Clarisa's living room.

"What now?" she asks finally, but doesn't wait for an answer. Instead she begins to undress.

He feels suddenly compelled to tell her his name. It doesn't seem to register; instead she turns so he can help her undo the top clasp of her yellow dress. He does, hands hardly trembling, heart pounding at the absurdity of it, this strange woman in her underwear, bouncing her weight from one short, slim leg to the other. She seems very nice. Her black hair falls to her shoulders. Nothing could be less erotic.

"So?" she says, and he realizes he no longer has the right to refuse. That choice is not available to him.

"So," he says.

It's over a few minutes later.

While she dresses, Hernán picks the cushions off the floor

and rearranges them on the sofa. There's a heaviness to his gestures, a certain hopelessness.

She turns once more so he can help with the last clasp of her dress. She lifts her hair again and offers her back to him. A soft rain taps the roof. The skin of her neck is tinted blue in the afternoon light.

"I'm a friend of Clarisa's. Just so you know. You were wonderful yesterday at the Versailles."

"Thank you," Hernán says, defeated.

She's about to go. He wants her to go.

Then: "Do I pay you or just work it out with Clarisa later?"

⚊ LIFE VERSUS ANARCHY ⚊

For a long time, Hernán thought his marriage could be saved. More than that: he knew it could be. This was factual certainty, something scientists could prove in a laboratory. At the same time, if he were honest, he knew it wasn't the pertinent question, not the one he should be asking.

Did he *want* it to be saved?

It tormented him. He woke up wondering, and carried it with him all day. As he made breakfast; when he walked Aurelio to school across the River; at the university, even as he lectured before a roomful of students, even as the words spilled out automatically, his mind was elsewhere. If his marriage was his life, then every moment had to be interrogated. *Is this worth saving?*

How about this?

Or this?

Then he realized that *not being sure* was answer enough. Then he realized Adri wasn't sure either. He felt their combined uncertainty floating above them as they pretended to sleep. In the dark early-morning hours, as they lay in bed, silent, he could tell she was thinking it too.

Then he knew it was over.

But still, Hernán didn't leave. People far better than him in every way have skated to their graves stuck in bad relationships, such is the coercive power of inertia. *Maybe we can make it,* he thought. *Perhaps the routines will carry us through.* They had a home, after all. They had Aurelio.

But in his heart, Hernán knew it was coming. She was stronger than he was. Less enamored of habit. He knew he'd never have the strength to walk away, but began to suspect that she would. He could sense it in her manner, the way her jaw set before she answered him, the flatness of her speech. He wasn't surprised exactly. When it happened, finally, her eyes were trained on him with a directness he'd never seen, her face expressionless, almost lawyerly. He knew this was the moment—*panic*—and made some sort of plea, something about how much he loved her, how much he loved Aurelio, how they were a family, in spite of it all—when she interrupted him, shaking her head.

"You're a good father, Hernán. You've been a good father to my son."

He felt a sudden surge of gratitude, even hope.

"But that's not enough. You still have to be a good husband."

A strand of black hair had fallen in her eyes, and now she tucked it behind her ear.

"What do you mean?" he managed.

"You expect me to be grateful. Like you saved me. Saved us. Like I don't have the right to complain because you're doing us some kind of favor by raising my son." She gritted her teeth. "You aren't."

"I know," he said.

"Do you?" She shook her head, answering her own question. She sighed like someone setting down a heavy weight. "I let you into our life. I did *you* the favor."

Now, in the port city, that seems truer than ever. There was no greater gift, and now it's gone.

His debasement begins in earnest. He's a kept man, unemployed, at least officially, but suddenly working harder than ever.

"Oh no," he'd said that day Clarisa's friend mentioned money. He'd answered without hesitation, a fact that still surprised him. Perhaps he'd known what was happening all along—he certainly should have. The scale of his vanity was suddenly clear to him.

"Just work it out with Clarisa."

The strange woman smiled. "Of course."

Then: ten days, six visitors. He never confronts Clarisa. Ten more days, and he's stopped counting the women. He watches Clarisa for a sign, but she hasn't changed. She has no need to. Hernán makes love to the women on the sofa in the living room. Some afternoons he's more inspired than others. Some women desire him with genuine passion; others are more reserved, their bodies letting him know they don't expect much in the way of acrobatics. They grunt and moan politely, nothing more. The sofa is in frankly terrible shape, the cushions flipped over so many times, he doesn't remember which sides are supposedly clean. On a few occasions he's had to move the coffee table against the wall, to make space on the floor for a particularly energetic visitor.

By now it's June, and his strength is waning. Hernán is exhausted. Some afternoons, he considers leaving the house, scattering into the streets before any visitor arrives.

But he doesn't, of course. He'll never leave. In fact, he's still there. See him: sleeping in the storage room that Josué transformed for him when he returned, sitting up in his twin bed to peer out the tiny window that faces the alley behind the house. He doesn't come out in the morning until the house is empty, Clarisa to the boutique, Josué to the port. He hears them talking at breakfast. He hears them laughing. And still the women visit, and Hernán does his job. He is diligent, dutiful, though he no longer expects any reward. In the evenings, Clarisa brings him a plate of food, a glass of juice, which she leaves on a tray by the door. He's free to go whenever he wants, they tell him. They're good to him, and he knows they mean it.

"You did well today," Clarisa whispers through the door. "We're proud of you. Aren't we, Josué?"

ACKNOWLEDGMENTS

First, I'd like to explain the title story of this collection and where it came from. "The King Is Always Above the People" references an image of a hanging, and is inspired by a cartoon by Ardeshir Mohassess. The original can be found in the excellent *Life in Iran: The Library of Congress Drawings*.

I'm indebted to the many friends who read versions of these stories along the way, offering advice, ideas, and the occasional pep talk: Vinnie Wilhelm, Adam Mansbach, Josh Begley, Lila Byock, Mark Lafferty, Joe Loya, and Rabih Alameddine.

Thank you to my colleagues and friends at Radio Ambulante, especially Camila Segura. Working so closely with you these last several years has helped shape the way I think about stories.

Thank you to my editor, Laura Perciasepe, for your patience and unflagging support.

Lastly, thank you to my family, especially my wife, Carolina. Without you, this book, and most of the things that make me happy, would simply not exist. Gracias, mi amor.